Not a Good Fit

Adam Hulse

NOT A GOOD FIT AT THIS TIME

AN ADAM HULSE COLLECTION

All work copyright Adam Hulse

Author retains all rights to published work

Editing and formatting – Damien Casey
Cover design and image – Laura Cathcart aka
Cutfingers
Published by Infested Publishing

Introduction

The title for this collection has been complimented more than any other book I've released.

It's no coincidence those speaking up have been fellow writers. From my point of view, I want to be clear about something; it is not aimed towards publishers, agents etc. That would be a pretty dumb move even by my standards. Although it is a phrase I have received via email on many occasions from industry professionals. I need you to understand that there is no ill feeling on my behalf. It's just a statement which has stuck with me because I think it perfectly sums up the human condition. A horror writer desperately trying to fit into a community, a writer hoping their work is good enough, a person wanting to find their place in society. The crushing sense of pressure to fit into a pigeonhole is something I've had an aversion to since my teenage years as a punk who felt he was locked out from the social life he wanted. Fitting in? Belonging? There's true horror there, my friends.

My writing journey began during the lockdown procedures COVID sent our way. I knew my mental health was going to suffer badly if I didn't do something productive with my time in isolation, so I started typing. There are stories from those early days right through to one I wrote this year. The sporadic nature to word counts is due to the initial calls but at least you get variety. It has been clear from revisiting the original drafts that the publishers were correct in their assessment that my work wasn't good enough to be accepted. I've enjoyed seeing things from their point of view and it has allowed me to be ruthless with the reworking of all the stories within this collection. I've used every single lesson I have learned so far to get these stories to a standard I'm now proud of. I still believe in these stories, and I'm sure I'd eventually find homes for them, but I worry I'd forget about them somehow, so this works best for me.

Most subgenres of horror are featured here as well as a little sci-fi and dark fantasy. I hope the mix is something you enjoy, and they have gone towards proving my versatility to... well, me!

That Ain't No Wayward Grizzly

Smoke signalled the death of their fire. It was enough to agitate Johnny's throat to coughing. He spat and cursed his luck at such an abrupt arrival into the waking world. Partly because the terrain had wiped him out and partly because he'd been having a wonderful dream about the mayor's daughter.

"Oh, Suzy," he sighed as he adjusted his heavy woollen pants and raised up on his elbow.

Johnny looked across at Bill who slept with his boots practically in the ashes of the campfire. As usual he was snoring so loudly his graying moustache twitched like a butterfly basking in sunshine. Johnny looked over to where young Henry should have been sleeping but there was no sign of him.

"Taking a piss, I expect," he grumbled.

Johnny about closed his eyes when a thought surged through him and sat him bolt upright.

Where are the horses?

John immediately pulled the repeater

from under his saddle, which he'd been using as a pillow, and stood up unsteadily. The sun hadn't battled over the horizon yet, but its promise of morning was close enough to bathe the plains in an unnatural gray light. Johnny shivered from a combination of the lack of fire and the unnatural occurrence of Henry and the horses going missing. There was no good reason for it as far as Johnny could figure, and that's what set his teeth to chattering.

"Bill?"

The man continued to snore like a wild boar.

"Bill, wake up, damn you!"

A loud snort interrupted the snoring and Bill addressed his friend without opening his eyes.

"What in the Hell has got into you to be hollering at such an ungodly hour?"

"How do you know what hour it is? You got your darn eyes closed!"

Bill sat up with all the elegance of a creaky chair.

"I know because it is, that's how!"

"By God, you vex me, Bill Jameson!"

Bill seemed cheered by the agitation he caused and attempted to rub the hangover from his eyes before looking around the camp.

"Where the Hell are the horses?" he suddenly yelped.

Johnny sagged at the shoulders and rolled his eyes.

"That's what I'm trying to tell you, idgit! Now keep your damn voice down."

Bill turned at the waist and retrieved his Colt revolver from beneath his blanket. When he stood it was on legs twice as shaky as Johnny's.

"Where's Henry?" he whispered.

A snapping sound reached them before being carried away on the constant wind of the plains. Johnny shook his head grimly and pointed his rifle to where the scrub got denser around a large rock formation. Bill nodded in agreement and the pair set out on unsteady legs to investigate. Johnny recalled terrible tales of Mexican horse thieves, while Bill swallowed hard at the thought of a wayward grizzly.

The smell hit them like a hammer to the face. It was horse meat, shit, and something sweet which made the assault all the more nauseating. Johnny and Bill were stopped in their tracks by the barrage and their eyes watered as they glanced nervously at one another. The moment to run presented itself as something comfortable and uncomplicated. Johnny leaned into it for a moment but then shook his head and fixed to spit onto the parched ground. Except he was dry from sleep, and the spittle lazily collided with his stubbled chin. Embarrassed, Johnny turned from Bill and wiped it away with the back of his sleeve.

"We owe it to Henry to look."

Bill nodded somberly and pointed his

revolver to a large boulder.

"Reckon the smell is coming from behind that there rock."

"I reckon so," Johnny replied in a small voice he didn't recognise.

They moved as though through the fog of a nightmare. The hum of an enormous amount of insects almost deterred them from walking around the boulder but they persevered.

"By God," Bill whimpered.

Johnny opened his mouth but shut it in case it gave him away. The sight before them was illogical and it cruelly insisted, they looked longer than they wished so they could make sense of it all. Their horses were piled atop each other in twisted shapes only achieved by death. Johnny tilted his head and saw all three had been hollowed out and shore of their fat and innards. Bill coughed back nausea at the side of him and Johnny flinched at the sound. Their eyes roamed the pile of death like the flies which feasted greedily there. Young Henry's face could be seen in the mess of it all. He looked surprised to be lying in such a compromising position and Johnny felt the pinprick sting of tears frame his eyes. The young man's ribcage was exposed and the last of his meat mingled with that of the horses in an obscene manner. A beetle wandered out from inside Henry's bloodless mouth and Johnny reeled away and dry-heaved at his boots.

"Son of a bitch!" Bill cried at the sky as he followed.

Both men staggered away to their camp as though lost. Johnny had just about composed himself when the worst sound the men had ever heard tore its way across the land. It was somewhere between a blood curdling scream of anguish, and a primal roar of defiance. The din ripped the land as though it would crack the very ground their legs trembled upon. A silence followed which was alive enough to unnerve the hardiest of folk. Neither Bill nor Johnny fell into that category. They raced on through their camp and ignored their saddles and blankets as though they belonged to someone else.

"What the hell was that sound?" Bill huffed as he kicked up dust.

Johnny looked over his shoulder and scowled at his friend.

"Less talking and more running for our lives!"

"Can't we do both?"

Johnny appraised his friend's physique and hangover.

"I could, maybe."

"Now what in the hell is that supposed to mean, god damn you!"

Johnny carried on rushing from the camp and through the scrub, but Bill bustled on after him.

"I'm fixing to whip you!"

Johnny stopped and gave an exasperated groan.

"You can knock my teeth down my throat once we get to somewhere safe, ok?"

Then he set off jogging again.

"I just might," Bill called from behind him. "I just might!"

They ran for five more minutes before a second beastly cry threw some pace into their leaden legs. This time it came from the area where they'd made camp and the fury in the sound propelled Bill past Johnny.

"It's following us!"

Johnny sped up, mainly so he could needle his friend.

"Well, ain't you just the total package."

"What you mean by that?" Bill managed.

"Not only are you the toughest man in the whole west, but you're the smartest too!"

Bill growled at Johnny, and they ran for a few minutes more.

Johnny took to needling his good buddy when he was stressed. He figured it was reasonable seeing as he was being pursued on aching feet by a devilish creature.

"Well, go on genius! What's the plan?"

"I was following you!" Bill panted, aghast.

"That's what I figured," Johnny panted. "Now shut up and follow me some more!"

The pair ran on careful to avoid turning their ankles on the uncompromising terrain. There had been no more roars from behind them, but they knew something ungodly was in pursuit. They worried the silence just meant it was getting closer. Finally, as the men moved over a rise in the land, a series of small buildings came into view. The friends grinned at each other.

"You son of a bitch," Bill beamed.

Johnny took the praise any which way he could get it and ran on with a grin on his face and a flicker of hope in his heart.

***

Bannack was a town on the up. The promise of gold in the nearby hills had seen the hasty construction of a saloon with three rooms for rent sitting empty above it. Building materials were in the process of being transported across tough country so that miner's quarters could extend the street to accommodate close to one hundred miners. In six months' time Bannack would be unrecognizable, but as Bill and Johnny blustered to a dusty standstill, they were underwhelmed. A rickety shack stood off to one side while a half constructed general store stood waiting for its owners to finish the job. Johnny looked over to the saloon and noted the paint had barely dried. Yet, four stout horses were tied up out front, so the pair ran to it. They crashed through the swinging doors with the grace of rampaging bulls and were met with the sight of a skinny barkeep with slicked back, black hair. He wore a smart shirt, and his sleeves were pinned up. It was clear he took offense at the two red-faced cowboys entering his saloon. Yet it wasn't he who cursed them out.

"What a damn racket!"

Both Bill and Johnny looked to the source of the voice. The owners of the four horses outside were sitting around a small table playing cards and draining whiskey. They were a rough looking bunch and Johnny figured out quickly to not upset them anymore than their noisy entrance already had. He went to remove his hat but realized he must have lost it during their escape. Johnny cursed inwardly and nodded politely at the men at the table.

"Apologies, gentlemen," he said before moving to the bar.

Johnny could feel the men bristling and staring openly at him as he passed by. His stomach clenched in anticipation of the upcoming dispute. He was amazed at how far away the body of young Henry and their horses seemed now they were in the saloon. How strange a sensation to think of the beast's howls now that dangerous men were on his back. Johnny arrived at the bar with Bill at his side.

The barkeep's face appeared to be marked with nerves from catering to the gambling brutes. It was a display which did nothing to appease Johnny's bubbling guts.

"We need your help," he asked the barkeep in a low voice.

Before the man could respond, the telltale sound of chair legs dragging over the wooden floor came from behind them.

"I'm not done talking to you!"

Bill visibly winced at Johnny's side and the latter had no choice but to turn and take his medicine.

The standing man was red in the face and his large moustache twitched with anger. He was stocky and his clenched fists looked capable of ironing Johnny out in five seconds flat. Johnny noted one of his companions already had his own hand hovering near the decorative handle of his revolver. He was surprised to see he was still holding his own rifle. The fright of the morning had seen him taken leave of his senses. Hell, he was lucky to have not been shot on sight, running into a saloon with a repeater in his hands. Bill hastily crammed his pistol into his belt and Johnny placed his rifle onto the bar. He ignored the look of revulsion from the barkeep and returned his focus to self-preservation.

"Listen, fellas," he started.

"No, you listen to me, you little pipsqueak!" the man raged.

Johnny's face reddened but he swallowed his anger so the man could have his say.

"You think it's ok to rush in here with your weapons drawn? Disturbing me and the boys while we're trying to relax after a hard night."

Johnny didn't want to think what would constitute as a hard night for such a rough outfit.

"Well, cat got your tongue?"

"No, it's not ok, but let me explain."

The man's eyes widened a notch.

"Are you cussing me out, boy?"

"No, God no!"

The man looked at his companions and a flash of communication registered from one set of eyes to the next until the entire table was unified in some dastardly plan.

"Do you think he's cussing me out, Tom?"

All eyes moved to the man whose hand teetered near his gun. The man had small black eyes which reminded Johnny of a snake. He smirked and looked right through the men at the bar.

"Oh, I just can't be sure, Frank," he replied in a gruff but playful voice.

"Hmm, what about you, Wesley?"

Johnny felt hotter than he had done when he was running across the plains. The men were clearly enjoying the intimidation they were doling out. Wesley was a gaunt specimen with gray hair and a rope scar around his neck which sent a shiver up Johnny's spine.

"I'd say it's possible," Wesley grinned.

Johnny opened his mouth to protest but Frank fixed him with a look so black he expected to see stars in it.

"What say you, Pat?"

The room turned to look at the last man at the table. He still observed his cards as though he were reading a book. Johnny figured he might be slow. Pat tilted his head to get a better look at Johnny and the latter thought he was probably looking at Frank's older brother. The man's bloodshot eyes appraised him as though he was looking for some measure of value or courage. Johnny regretted putting his rifle on the bar behind him.

"I'd say he looks the type," Pat sneered.

Frank's eyes and mouth grew wider in a theatrical gesture as though his brother's word was akin to God Himself. Bill had had enough.

"We don't have much time!" he blurted out.

"Ain't that the truth!" Frank retorted.

The table erupted in cruel laughter.

"There's something out there-"

Frank cut Bill off with a total lack of interest.

"Where are you two idiots from to think you can barge in here like that?"

It was Johnny's turn to blurt words out and he was filled with instant regret.

"Abilene."

"Abilene, eh?" Frank guffawed. "Maybe we should pay Abilene a visit some time, boys."

The table echoed the ghoulish laughter and Johnny and Bill used the break to shoot each other anxious looks.

A dark shadow suddenly passed by the window behind Frank and his crew. Johnny and Bill fell back against the bar in terror. The sound of four guns being drawn was sobering. Frank and his men all aimed their guns at the bar.

"Tell me why we shouldn't fill you two fellas full of lead?"

Before either man could find an adequate answer, the horses tied up outside began snorting and fussing at a volume which had all looking towards the window.

"Wesley, go and check what has the horses so spooked."

The lean man stood from the table and moved for the door.

"Don't go out there," Johnny warned.

"You, shut your damn mouth!" Frank warned.

"Please, we gotta get out of here!" Bill whimpered.

Frank raised his gun higher, so it aimed directly at Bill's face.

17

"So help me God, I will paint that bar with your brains if you don't start talking straight!"

The doors swung shut behind Wesley.

"Something killed our horses and our friends."

"Bullshit! You got someone out there stealing our horses while you distract us, boy?"

"No! We're telling the truth, I swear."

The horses were braying louder than before until falling abruptly silent. Frank scowled at the development but continued his questioning having enjoyed the taste of power.

"Where did your friend get kilt?"

"About five miles east of here."

Frank moved his gun to Johnny's face in response.

"There ain't nothing out there but scrub. The hell were you doing out there?"

"We'd made camp there."

"You looking to take our gold?" Frank accused as he sent spittle flying.

"No, God, no!" Johnny spluttered. "We're heading east out to find real ranch work that pays decent like."

Frank was about to respond when Wesley crashed back through the saloon doors. A collective gasp came from all within as they saw the man's arms had been removed. Blood gushed like it was being poured from a bucket, and Wesley slipped in it and landed dead. A familiar roar came from the street outside and both Bill and Johnny knew those horses were nothing more than a pile of meat now.

The large dark shape moved past the window again but this time it moved slowly as though taunting those within the saloon. Frank let out a war cry and he and his men peppered the window with bullets. Johnny retrieved his repeater from the counter and was half-dragged behind the bar by Bill.

"You can't come behind here," the barkeep yelped.

"Shut the Hell up," Bill hissed.

The barkeep threw his hands in the air as Bill practically put the tip of his revolver up his nostril.

"Now get your gun and help us live through this thing, God damn you!"

The barkeep fumbled under the bar and retrieved a double barrel shotgun of such poor condition it looked as though it posed more of a threat to the person wielding it rather than those at the business end. Bill looked at the relic in disgust and the smart dressed barkeep looked away in shame.

Frank and Tom paced towards the bar with their pistols raised.

"What the Hell did you boys get us mixed up in?" Frank screamed.

"We don't know!" Johnny yelled back in frustration. "We tried to tell you!"

"You didn't tell us shit!"

"Is it a grizzly?" Pat asked as he peered

out of the window.

"Come away from there, Pat," Frank ordered.

"I can't see anything out there but poor Wesley's blood."

"I said get away from the damn-"

Before Frank could finish his sentence, a heavily muscled arm, which was covered in tufts of gray fur, reached through the broken glass, and grabbed at Pat's head. The hand enveloped his entire skull. Johnny noted the claws looked like oversized human nails, but there was nothing human standing outside that saloon. The beast tightened its grip and Pat's head collapsed in on itself like a piece of rotten fruit. The sound reminded Johnny of a mallet hitting a fence post and he was caught up in a memory of when he and Bill had been paid to do a hefty amount of new fencing up at the duke's farm. Brain and blood wormed through the gaps between the killing hand as Frank emitted a sorrowful cry. Johnny lifted his rifle and fired a round which ricocheted off the window frame. Tom coolly aimed and fired. The shot tore through the brutish arm causing it to release Frank's dead brother. His killer howled in rage and Johnny felt his legs nearly giving out beneath him.

For a moment there was a heavy silence as the men watched the window and saloon doors anxiously. Then the steady sound of both Frank and Tom frantically reloading their guns could be heard. A single bullet fell from Frank's mitt, and it rolled noisily towards the door. The men watched it with pained expressions as though they were trying to sneak past a guard dog. It came to a stop in Wesley's blood and the sound was replaced by the scrape of claws scratching on the wood between door and window. Johnny thought of the bastardized fingernails and shuddered.

"It's playing with us," Bill whispered.

Even Frank and Tom looked nervous now and they withdrew further from the door. The barkeep put the relic of a gun on the bar and began fumbling around. He grabbed a nearby broom and snapped the handle under his boot. The men watched as he hastily tied a dish rag around it.

"What in the hell are you doing?" Frank hissed.

The barkeep ignored the question and instead poured a little liquor on the rag and fumbled in his pockets for a small box of matches. Johnny and Bill nodded approval as the rag slowly ignited to create a torch. Even Frank seemed satisfied and returned to aiming at the door. The barkeep stood holding the torch proudly, but the flame highlighted the copious volume of sweat on his brow.

"We got a plan?" Frank whispered.

"The door only allows for us to leave one at a time and that thing will cut us down with ease," Johnny put in.

"So, we need to bring it to us," Frank sighed.

"Then we can all open fire on it all at once," Bill stated in a low tone.

"Leave it outside, I say!" the barkeep blurted out.

"Don't you understand, you idgit?" Johnny scolded. "That bastard ain't going anywhere."

"He's right," Tom grunted. "We need to draw it in here."

He took confident strides towards a dusty old piano which sat up against the wall in a neglected state. Tom moved his long leather duster to the side so he could sit on the small stool. He lifted the lid to reveal a row of stained black and white keys hiding under a coat of cobwebs. Frank crept to the space between the piano and the saloon doors. Bill and Johnny joined him there with their weapons raised. Frank looked over his shoulder and nodded once for Tom to begin.

The gunslinger expertly began to play the introduction to "My Old Kentucky Home." He winced due to the piano being badly in need of tuning and cast a hateful look at the barkeep. Once more, the man behind the bar looked away in shame. Tom licked his cracked lips in preparation of singing the first verse when the saloon doors were smashed open as their hunter made its entrance. Three of the men pissed their pants at the sight before them and the piano abruptly cut out. The creature's height ensured it had to stoop to walk through the doorway on the thick, crooked legs of a hound. Its bare feet were hairy, the size of shovels, and they crushed Wesley's corpse beneath them. Scars covered a barrel-like body which was not dissimilar to a grizzly bear. Grey fur was torn out in clumps which made for an obscene torso. The beast's arms were almost to the floor, and all in the room had already bore witness to their power. Any similarities to any known animal were murdered by the lump which sat upon the creature's heavy shoulders. It looked like four human heads had been thrown into each other and melted in a fused state of extraordinary evil.

The stupor of being in front of such demonic terror caused the men to hesitate and it was the only invitation the beast required. Its left arm swiped with surprising speed and collided with both Johnny and Bill. They were swatted to the floor like gnats, the impact snapped Johnny's rifle and broke Bill's nose. The beast opened its enormous mouth to reveal two dagger-like teeth embedded in black gums. It drove down onto Frank and his head and shoulders disappeared into the abyss. Frank squeezed the trigger of his pistol in a reflex action, and from his place on the floor, Johnny saw the bullet tear through the barkeep's throat. His last sight of the man was as he went crashing backwards into the shelves of liquor. There was a whoosh as his torch kissed the booze. Bill grabbed Johnny with one hand as he held his nose together with the other.

"Head for the stairs!" he gurgled.

Johnny struggled to a standing position on unsteady legs as Tom began expertly firing at the beast. He heard Frank's body slop to the floor as he staggered to the staircase which was accessed to the side of the bar. The flames were snaking off in all directions as though a second beast had entered the room. Johnny ran to collect the old double-barrel shotgun from the bar before it was cremated along with the barkeep. He turned to see both Bill and Tom firing at the demon which inched closer under the burden of pain.

For a moment, Johnny felt as though the creature was going to succumb but then it made a chopping motion with its right arm and Tom's head spiralled away from his body. Bill took a few steps backwards and turned to Johnny.

"Run!" he screamed. "Get outta here!"

Johnny ran past the flames which were now licking the dry wooden ceiling. The first step creaked under his boot as he heard Bill grunt from behind him. He turned the corner of the staircase and caught sight of his friend's boots shuddering five feet from the floor as the beast picked him up with ease. Johnny didn't stick around to hear the wet chomps of feeding. He raced across the landing hoping to escape through a window. Johnny rattled the doorknobs presented to him, but all were locked. He thought of the keys in the burning bar below as heavy crashing came from the staircase. The beast came into view. It was covered in the blood and shit of its victims. Johnny wiped a sleeve over his eyes to the smoke and tears of his fallen friends. The creature moved clumsily in the tight space as it sought him out. Johnny raised the shotgun with a shaky arm but before he had a chance to pull the trigger the floor let out a tremendous groan. The combination of fire and the enormous weight of the demon saw it fall through a large section of the landing with a colossal crash.

It was a reprieve which Johnny didn't aim on wasting. He took a running jump over the hole in the floor and bounced off the wall at the top of the stairs. As he half-fell down the ruined steps, Johnny could hear the beast howling and flailing in the flames. Johnny looked sideways and saw it had crushed the bar beneath its mass. The creature's legs jutted out at irregular angles which told him they were broken. Johnny moved to escape the saloon, but the sight of Bill's ruined body stopped him in his tracks. His best friend had given his life for him to escape. Johnny felt the anger rise up like bile from a poisoned stomach. The shotgun hung heavy by his side. He turned to the flames to have his revenge just as the beast grabbed his left ankle. Johnny fell with a thud and his face was heavily splintered as he was dragged towards that giant mouth. He kicked out but the grip was too strong. With the last of his own strength, Johnny turned on his side and aimed both barrels of the barkeep's shotgun at the beast's hand. He pulled both triggers just as the hand tugged at his leg. The blast not only obliterated all of the demon's fingers, but also sent half of Johnny's foot spraying through the air.

Both Johnny and the beast howled at the flame covered ceiling. Johnny recovered first and free of his captive, began crawling on his elbows towards the saloon door. He'd made it past the piano when he heard the crippled beast begin crawling in pursuit. Johnny refused to look but he could hear the sizzling of the creature's skin and the snarling behind him.

I hope you're hurting, you son of a bitch, he thought.

Yet he too was trailing thick blood in his wake and dizziness intensified with every inch he progressed. By the time Johnny was outside the burning saloon, pain, exhaustion, and blood loss were just about to overcome him. He rolled onto his back in defeat and stared up at a lone cloud. The sound of the warm breeze accompanied the noise of the demon dragging itself closer. Johnny squinted at the bright sky until the beast's wide-open mouth blocked every sight from view. He braced himself for oblivion, but a shotgun blast caused him to flinch instead. A large chunk of the creature's head turned to vapor, and the beast slowly fell away from Johnny as though it were being deflated.

"Well, I must say, father, this has been quite the hunt."

"Very true, dear. Now let's get that boy to a doctor," the mayor's voice called out from nearby.

A shadow fell across his face and Johnny looked up at his saviour. The sun created a halo over her golden hair.

"Suzy?"

The mayor's daughter smiled down on Johnny.

"I had the most wonderful dream about you last night," he confessed before passing out.

NOTES

This is the only story which I wrote specifically for this collection. Selfishly it was to scratch the itch I had to write something within a genre I love. I'm a huge fan of Westerns and it's been fun to see the trend of splatter westerns rising up in popularity. I did have another splatter-western short story (which had been rejected for publishing), but I intend on developing it into a novella as a close friend said it had the "legs" to do so. I own every Cormac McCarthy book, and most by Larry McMurtry, and although it probably doesn't show, I have been greatly influenced by their work. Even if it is just emitting a whimsical sigh after closing one of their books.

The point is that it can be tough going for a Brit to traverse the barren plains and lively saloons without feeling like a complete tourist. I hope my years of devouring the books of the aforementioned superstars has served to make my story tolerable.

Valley of the Blood Shadows

Bright morning sunshine beamed over the cramped tent. Mike and Nicola awoke with hungover groans and the synchronicity of Siamese twins due to the confines of the double sleeping bag. Nicola rubbed her eyes before staring sleepily at the blue nylon stretched above them. The headache pulsed in her temples, drumming steadily towards a bad mood. Mike had promised the double sleeping bag, which he had stolen from his parents, would provide the wild night their teenage hormones craved. Instead, they had drank too much cider and argued over stupid jealous nonsense before embarking on the worst sleep of their lives. Nicola cursed herself for lying to her mum about staying at Michelle's last night. The disappointment hung over them both like the clammy plastic smell the tent was filled with. Mike smiled weakly and moved the fringe from his eyes. When his girlfriend's mood had been measured, he unzipped the sleeping bag.

"I need a piss."

Nicola watched in silence as her boyfriend hit his head on the top of the tent before fumbling with the tent's zip. Both cringed at the noise of the metal teeth and the blinding light of a new day which followed. Nicola's mood improved slightly at the sight of Mike stumbling outside wearing only his boxer shorts and Nirvana t-shirt. Maybe something could be salvaged from this disaster date after all.

Mike aimed his urine at a nettle, which immediately splashed back onto his bare feet. Another example of camping being something he now found overrated.

"For God's sake!"

As he shook his wet foot out, he looked up at the canopy the trees had created above him. The July sky was already a deep blue, and the sun promised another long, sweltering day. Against the nagging disappointment and dehydration he felt, Mike couldn't help but smile at the tranquillity of the moment. The smile faded when the atmosphere seemed to change somehow. When Mike took a few more careful steps away from the nettles, he realised what was bugging him. The birds had stopped singing. They had been trilling the whole time the sun had surfaced; but now that Mike was standing in the woods, he heard not a single call. He turned back towards the tent so he could see if Nicola had noticed, but a sound somewhere behind froze him in place. It was the lazy whistle of an adult trying to get someone's attention. Mike's hairs stood erect where his outfit allowed, and he shot a tentative look over his shoulder. Nobody stood among the trees, but as he rushed back to Nicola, the whistle called to him once more. The tent came into view and Mike felt his stomach flip. Sunshine picked out the dark stains on the newly ripped material.

That's not my tent. Please don't be my tent.

Silence hummed in Mike's ears as he peered through a flap in the material. Someone had smeared something all over the floor of the tent and the first thought he had was his dad was going to kill him. What at first glance looked like a white latex glove was quickly realised to be a bloodless hand.

That's not her. That's not Nicola.

A buzzing of silence raged in Mike's ears like the flies which were already seeking out the meat in the tent. The same whistle which had spooked him called out again and Mike scrambled away in the opposite direction. Branches lashed at his face and thorns clawed at his shins as he used all his speed to zigzag around the trees. Mike knew these woods like the back of his hand and rushed to the nearby stream. A small wooden footbridge was the perfect hiding place, so he rushed under it. The water was only ankle deep, but the cold of it took the last of his laboured breath away. Mike had to crane his neck to fully fit under the bridge, which was six feet long and four feet in width. Thankfully, the overgrown banks of the stream created natural cover either side of him. His cuts stung in the water, but Mike was glad to think of something other than the contents of the tent.

Birdsong had returned to the area and Mike allowed tears to finally flow.

Nicola. What am I going to do? What am I going to tell everyone?

Mike looked to the left at the rays of golden sunshine falling beautifully onto the rippling water. Pollen danced there. For a moment he felt as though his girlfriend was still with him. A thud atop the bridge caused Mike to flinch in terror. The sunlight was quickly forgotten as the sound of slow footsteps above told him someone else was with him. Mike held his breath as dust fell through the cracks in the wood. Finally, the footsteps moved away, and he let out a slow shaky sigh. Then a familiar whistle blew onto the back of his neck.

***

Detective Alan Turner grunted as he hefted himself out of the car. Already self-conscious of what age was doing to him, he refused to look at his younger and more capable partner.

"Do we need to talk about your diet again?"

Turner mentally cursed and slowly turned his head to glance across at Detective

Joy Wainwright. Although only four years into her current role, Wainwright was already at Turner's level even though he was nearing retirement age. The only pleasure Turner extracted from their working relationship was witnessing his partner turn her destructive attention onto a more fitting victim. Usually when another detective attempted flirtation, but mainly it boiled over if someone asked her to smile. Detective Wainwright used her index finger to temporarily move one side of her blonde bob behind her ear. The only purpose of this action was so Turner could better see her smirk over the roof of their car. Wainwright had a lot of time for the grumpy veteran she had been thrown in with, it was just too much fun breaking his balls.

Detective Turner was about to rise to the bait and defend his kebab addiction when there was a commotion at the taped-off entrance to Sankey Hill Park. Turner and Wainwright ignored the wail of a parent, the stares from local press, and the nods from the two uniformed officers attempting to keep the public from entering the area.

"Has the Blood Shadow struck again?"

The detectives raced away from the nearest reporter before Turner shot Wainwright a confused look.

"Some kids discovered the bodies and uploaded footage to three separate social media platforms."

"Jesus."

The pair moved from the main path in silence with a swish of long grass the only sound to penetrate the warm air.

Forensics methodically worked around the crime scene; their protective suits giving them the appearance of ghosts which moved from tree to tree.

"The Blood Shadow murders were twenty years ago," Turner announced.

Wainwright stopped walking towards the ripped tent and waited for her partner. The famous case had been way before her time, but she'd read about it and even seen a press photograph of a young Detective Turner. He'd been wearing a look of deep trauma which would be more fitting as a death mask. The killer had never been apprehended and Wainwright noticed present day Turner had once more donned the mask.

"I'm sure it's just some idiot copycat," she tried.

Detective Turner grunted, furrowed his brow, and paced towards the tent.

The identification of the meat within was relayed to them by the nearest ghost but Turner didn't hear. Instead, he looked off towards a clearing which the sun launched its powerful beams into. A large white object lay on the ground there, highlighted by the golden rays. Turner felt he was suddenly overheating and absent-mindedly removed his jacket as he wandered away from the tent. He balled the material in his hand and walked in a dream-like trance towards the clearing. There was a small flag in the ground next to the object, but Turner didn't need to see the forensic catalogue to recognise what it was. He'd known the large paint canvas would be at the scene from the moment the reporter had mentioned the Blood Shadow. Turner looked down at the stretched figure painted onto the canvas knowing it had been painted with the blood of the victims.

Early on in the Blood Shadow murders they had thought the killer had been painting an impression of the latest victim. A macabre still life. However, while working on the fourth case, Turner had been standing with his back to the sun when observing the latest piece of "art" and his shadow had almost fit perfectly into the crimson silhouette. Detective Turner now felt the same dizzying sensation from twenty years earlier when he realised, he was looking at the killer's self-portrait.

The heat of the day seemed to increase with every minute and Turner had to close his eyes to steel himself against the feeling of faintness. Flies bounced around him in a collective which sounded like an engine and when he looked down again the stretched figure appeared to be wavering in the hazy heat of the day. The flies' volume increased to a climatic roar until everything was completely silent. Detective Turner realised the birdsong and bustle of his colleagues had also ceased.

Oh God, no. Please not again.

No matter how much he begged, the one sound he prayed wouldn't occur punctuated the silence. A man's whistle was calling to him. The same mocking sound he'd heard on numerous occasions all those years ago had returned. It was a sound which the rest of his team had said was in his head and he'd been forced to drop it. Yet there it was again. A whistle, like some devil trying to get his attention, beckoned from the nearby trees.

The two nearest forensic technicians had been dispatched in complete silence and Turner whimpered as he turned to see their exposed ribcages and lungs. He ran to warn his partner but before he raced past a decapitated forensic photographer, Turner knew he was too late. Detective Joy Wainwright was nowhere to be seen at first. It was the steady patter of blood on the destroyed tent below which told Turner to look up. There she was mouth open in agony and impaled on a large branch some thirty feet in the air. Turner wept as the whistle called from somewhere behind him. Twigs snapped close by, and he froze until he felt a warm breath move the hair on the back of his head.

Twenty Years Later

The Sankey Valley housing project had been built atop a massacre. Trees and earth bulldozed away once the council had sold off the park. The unsolved murders of Detectives Turner and Wainwright along with six members of the Merseyside forensic team had sent shockwaves through a community already reeling from the gruesome deaths they'd been investigating. Stories had been vague at first but quickly evolved into tall tales which undermined the severity of the case. After all, who wanted to believe one detective had been found high in a tree while the other had his limbs smashed and tied in a bow? No, better to stick to the facts officially reported of a copycat killer going on a kill spree which was over no sooner than it had started. Still, the community had baulked at the prospect of living on grounds so rich in blood. Until the luxurious estate had begun to take shape and, "actually it looks lovely there, doesn't it?"

Tom had heard the stories of course, who hadn't? There had been a barbeque not two months ago where neighbours had swapped details like a ghost story over the smell of cheap meat and lager. He smirked now as he mowed his wonderful green lawn. Poor Jane from two houses down had been scared out of her mind when Stu had jumped from behind the wheelie bins. Tom looked up at the blue sky and felt the tension of the working week leaving his shoulders. His mind was on the beer he had waiting for him in the fridge as he turned the lawnmower to do another lap. Tom failed to notice the arterial blood sprayed on the inside of the patio doors.

The noise of the petrol engine drowned out the whistle which called for him.

<u>NOTES</u>

This one hasn't changed much since it was rejected, but I can see now that it didn't fit the call as well as I thought at the time. I think sometimes we fall into the trap of getting a moment of inspiration and running away with it even when it takes us further away from the submission call. It was quite a general call, but I know for a fact I could have got it closer to what was being asked of those who were sending in work. All that being said, I'm happy with how this turned out. I'd been dying to write something with a police investigation edge to it and enjoyed the interplay between the old and young detectives. I wanted a really gritty crime feel to be devoured by a growing horror theme similar to Candyman or The First Power movie.

The whistle of our unseen killer is actually based on a true event which happened to me and a group of friends back in my teen years. We were supposed to be at a party, but a falling out between friends meant that four of us were stranded with nowhere to sleep. So, because it was summer, we decided to sleep in the Sankey Valley Park which is a local woodland near where I grew up. We had no camping equipment so of course we couldn't get ourselves comfortable even to sleep so we moved from place to place. During a lull in our conversations, a single whistle pierced the silence. It was around 4am and we were all spooked. After a few nervous comments the whistle sounded again, but nobody showed themselves. We decided to move on and left the park and walked ten minutes to a different park. The lack of sleep had us paranoid as hell, but we finally settled down. Until of course, the sound of the same whistle had us all jumping up in panic. Needless to say, we spent the rest of those early morning hours pacing up and down the streets while constantly looking over our shoulder.

Let Me Tell You About Your Father

On the eve of Christmas, I was awoken by a ghostly sob. My heart hammered a new tune.

"Leave him be!" I heard my aunt Maude cry.

Footsteps stumbled towards the bedroom where I had slept ever since my dear mother had passed two years ago. The door creaked open like a cat yawning, and I peered over my rough blankets at the silhouette swaying there in the gloom. For a moment I felt a strange sensation as though I was looking at my father; whom I had only seen in the crumpled photograph I had inherited from my mother after the sickness had taken her. His ship had been lost to the sea shortly before my birth. The man in the doorway moved slightly, so the oil lamp my aunt was carrying beat the shadows away to reveal my uncle Charles. I blinked sleepily and inwardly cursed my foolishness. Of course, the man looked similar to his own brother, but he was shorter and did not possess the striking blue eyes my mother had told me so much about.

"Come with me, child," Charles slurred.

I was quick to throw my cold feet over the side of my bed as I knew my uncle had a habit of being quick to lose his temper. Aunt Maude fussed in the background and when I tried to catch her eyes she looked away. Uncle Charles held his hand out for me to take, and although the gesture was not warm, I reached for it dutifully. My uncle's pinstriped suit was in disarray and his breath was hot with rum. While on the landing he swayed so violently it felt as though the whole house was teetering and I swear my feet momentarily left the rug. The movement was partnered with a sombre creak of wood.

Is this a dream? I fretted.

"Please, Charles," my aunt sobbed. "He's just a child."

With that my uncle snatched the lamp from my aunt's hand and leaned close to her puffy face.

"I promised them!" he hissed. "Wait in our room if you must, but I will see this through."

My mind raced as my aunt disappeared behind a slammed door and I descended the stairs with my uncle. We finally stopped in the moonlit hall, and I jumped in fright as my bare feet hit an icy cold puddle of water. I could see it was running from under the door that led to the front parlor. A splash of the water hit me in the face, and I was surprised to taste salt. My uncle sensed my hesitance.

"Come now, boy," he grunted and pulled at my arm.

The room as I knew it was gone. In fact, the very dimensions seemed to have changed as I felt the now familiar tilt pulling me one way and then another. Inexplicably the room was now flooded with grey looking water while ruin was all around. A gentle wave broke over my uncle and I before splashing up the damp walls of the hallway. I turned to look up at the face of my guardian for reassurance to steel me against the terror which bubbled within me. The sight of my uncle silently weeping made my legs buckle with fright. He sniffed once as though cold and waded out further into what had become of a once familiar room. I froze but again the pull of my uncle's grip was too much for me to resist.

"Uncle, please," I pleaded. "I don't understand."

I was soon up to my waist in the frigid water which sloshed up the walls all around us. My uncle remained stoney faced and silent. I was about to resume my questioning when the sound similar to the harbour bell began to toll all around us. Louder and louder, it became until my uncle's freezing cold hand began to hurt my fingers under his fearful grip. The lamp flickered and failed as were plunged into almost total darkness. Water still pressed against us, and I watched how moonlight broke through a crack in the curtains and danced on the ripples of movement. Uncle Charles let go of my hand for a moment and I felt the water try and pull me away.

"Uncle!" I cried out.

"Steel yourself, boy," came the reply as he tried to relight the lantern.

I teetered on the brink of falling forwards and then, just as suddenly, backwards. Something within me warned I would never rise back to the surface if I succumbed to the rising waves. The sea had visited the house and it wasn't about to soften its edges for a poor unfortunate such as myself. With one last desperate grunt, my uncle got the lantern burning again. His eyes filled me with dread as they were filled with nothing more than a void. What I had mistook for drunkenness was actually a state of deep shock. Still, my uncle grabbed my arm and dragged me in his wake towards where the back parlour used to be.

The door appeared swollen against its frame and the creak it emitted chilled my bones to the marrow. Even my uncle hesitated as he held the cold handle in his hand. He pressed his forehead into the panel and held it there. A tear ran down his nose and I watched it escape to the water which enveloped us.

"I'm sorry but I promised them such things," he wept before opening the door.

A man turned to watch our entrance. There

were shapes that moved unnaturally under the cape of his naval uniform. My uncle wept openly before hurrying out of the room. I heard the sloshing sound of his retreat but couldn't turn my eyes away from the figure before me. My father's striking blue eyes were dull now, but they took me in all the same.

NOTES

My one and only attempt (so far) at writing a more traditional gothic piece. I remember the call appealed to me because it would be a big test as it was pretty much the opposite of the style I had been writing up to that point. For some reason I thought I'd further test myself by writing in the first person which again was something I wasn't familiar with. Us writers are a masochistic bunch at times! Obviously, because I pushed myself and produced something I was proud of, I thought it was my God given right to have my submission published. The publishing God's disagreed!

On revisiting the story, I found it flawed, and once again it benefitted from me applying what I've learnt in the past couple of years to shape it into something better. The original call required a word count of 500 (I think) so as you can see, I've pretty much doubled that to give the story a more complete feel. I take my hat off to anyone who can achieve that to a high standard with 500 words and under. If I'm being honest, I feel my strengths lie elsewhere!

The title is something I'm still in love with. It has a depth to it and a pressing nature which gives a sense of some secret about to be revealed. A father and son dynamic is a complex one and that uncertainty is something I've played with by ramping up the creeping dread which runs away with the narrative. I suppose you want to know what happened to our central character once we leave him alone. Well, you tell me, dear reader. After all, you have as much power as I to shape that particular narrative. Maybe your imagination eclipses mine by some great measure.

Perhaps the family is cursed, and the promise made by the uncle is to sacrifice his nephew in order to save his own skin along with his wife's? Or maybe the offering is to keep the family in financial power? Is the man actually the boy's father, or has something from the deep claimed his appearance and memories when he was lost to the seas? I think one thing we can all agree on is there is no happy ending here. A cold embrace and saltwater kisses are most likely going to precede total darkness.

LEECH

<u>One</u>

Shadows crept across the ceiling of the hotel room that Jamie lay in. He wished he had the energy to stand at the window and watch the rush hour traffic crawl around below rather than watch the phantom-like reflections move across the ceiling. Jamie swallowed dryly as the thought of standing was enough to sucker punch him with another bout of nausea. The white bedsheet clung to the sheen that coated his skin and Jamie threw his left leg out from under its grip to try and regulate his fluctuating temperature. Thoughts floated back to the business convention he'd attended yesterday; Jamie ruefully considered the hot buffet he had visited afterwards with a body full of regret. He continued to stare at the light reflecting above the window as he became genuinely worried with how ill he was feeling.

There was a sudden sensation like wet suction on his exposed left leg accompanied by a sound like a wet "pop." Jamie simultaneously cried out and withdrew his left leg up to his chest. With his eyes wide open he scanned the side of the room that he had neglected for some time. His sickness was forgotten momentarily as a shot of adrenaline zipped through his system like electricity. Jamie sat up while still holding his leg in his arms, as though it were a vulnerable child, he was taking care of. He was amazed with how cold he suddenly felt given he was pretty sure he was running a high temperature. His stomach contracted and Jamie realised he had been holding his breath in fright. The fear within his guts intensified when on release his breath became mist in the suddenly freezing hotel room.

What the hell? he thought as he looked back to the window for reassurance.

The sun continued to burn, but before he could garner any calm from the ordinary, the room's door opened and then quickly slammed shut.

"Who's there?" he yelped.

The only sound was the distant chaos of rush hour traffic. Jamie's leg throbbed as a reminder, and he twisted it awkwardly to examine the side of his calf. To his horror there was a large mark there which looked like two friction burns running parallel. He was put in mind of the marks his first girlfriend used to put on his neck in high school. Jamie shuffled further back in the bed to use the headboard as an aid to getting fully upright. Nausea came to him quickly and it culminated in a spluttered dry retch which gave way to explosive coughing. Jamie wiped tears along his slim forearm and waited the convulsions out. Eventually, after sitting completely still for some time, he was able to begin to compose his thoughts.

Was someone in my room? he panicked.

Then his ears picked up a faint and tiny sound. Jamie again held his breath and tried to concentrate against the thumping of his own heartbeat. At first there was nothing, but then there it was again, and it was unmistakable. The noise of someone breathing. With eyes suddenly wide open, he realised the steady sound was coming from under the bed. Without hesitation, Jamie shot up, took one stride, and attempted to jump off the end of the bed so he could escape the room. Whether it was fatigue or the troublesome bed sheet, Jamie fell onto the worn carpet between the bed and the door. There was immediate movement from under the bed and Jamie rolled on his side to better see his pursuer. A balding man with sunken cheeks and a blank look in his eyes crawled slowly along on his elbows. Jamie felt frozen and the light in the room appeared to flicker even though he knew it wasn't dark outside yet. The man emitted a low groan and smiled at Jamie's exposed leg before reaching for it.

"Get away!" Jamie yelled and let a reflex kick connect with the man's hand.

The man opened his mouth wide in response; Jamie let out a gurgled scream at what he saw. There were no teeth within the man's mouth, just blackened and engorged gums. Jamie watched on in stunned silence as the old man traced his tongue around his mouth. What Jamie had believed to be gums squirmed in response, and he noticed the segmented rows that were highlighted by spittle. Jamie's leg throbbed in response as the man crawled closer from under the bed.

"No, no, no," he begged and rolled to a standing position.

Jamie took one last look at the old man, who stared back at him blankly, and slammed the door shut. He turned to run down the hotel corridors, but instead found they had been replaced with a dark tunnel. It was dimly illuminated by bunches of candles that lay sporadically along its length. Frantically he looked left and right before checking if the hotel door was still standing behind him. There it was, the same door for room 396 he had entered yesterday, except now it was set into stone rather than banal wallpaper. Jamie pressed his hand against the stone framing the door, it felt cold to the touch and looked ancient. His head was spinning, and he realised he was crying even though he didn't remember the start of the tears. A scream pierced the cold air and Jamie promptly vomited near his bare feet.

Two

Lucy had gone to sleep in her hotel bed and awoke on a stone slab. Nausea coiled around her stomach like a serpent and her vision blurred. Even so, she tried to take in her strange surroundings. The lighting was low so deep shadows made the task difficult, as did the dizziness which had a sensation similar to a bout of low blood pressure. There was a numbness to her feet which urged Lucy to wiggle her toes. The action provoked a murmur from the bottom of the rock bed she lay on. With aching temples, Lucy lifted her head so she could look down her sternum towards her legs. She sobbed at the sight presented to her. A gaunt forty-something man and an ancient looking woman with long white hair had their mouths attached to Lucy's feet.

The man had waxy skin and stared at her hungrily as he held the toes of her right foot firmly in his mouth. Lucy could not see much of the woman's face as she was too engrossed in sucking on the right heel that she gripped in her bony hands. Lucy screamed in fear and anger while kicking out with both of her legs. The couple reared up as though temporarily stunned and stood with eyes that mirrored the flickering of nearby candles. Lucy lay sickly still from the effort but hoped to God she had kicked the pairs teeth out. Shadows played across the faces of her attackers and Lucy found she was squinting to try and make sense of what she was looking at.

At first, she thought she had succeeded in dislodging some teeth but then her heart sank when the man turned his head slightly. Lucy looked at the black gums that pulsated in his mouth and felt her eyes opening wider and wider to try to take in what she was seeing. The old woman opened her mouth with what appeared to be great pride and Lucy saw the same slimy gums inside.

This is a nightmare, Lucy told herself as she turned her head away from the sight.

The couple again took hold of a leg each; but Lucy wasn't done fighting and so began shaking her legs as violently as her low energy levels would allow. A shadow blocked out half of the light in the room and a deep voice boomed out.

"Dubhthach, Boudica. Enough!"

Lucy tried to comprehend the ancient sounding words but drew a blank. Then the couple quickly retreated into the shadows, and she realised they must be their names. Slow and methodical footsteps interrupted her thoughts, she looked up to her right to see an impossibly tall man approaching the stone slab. His appearance stunned Lucy so much she abruptly stopped weeping and would have ceased breathing if she had been able. The man looked down and the two observed each other. He wore only a loin cloth and sandals which revealed not only a body that was devoid of hair, but one where every joint looked as though it had been endlessly stretched on a rack. His chest was sunken and heavily branded with symbols that Lucy did not recognise. She noted some of the symbols had also been painted onto the stone walls of the strange room.

Aside from the man's height, the most notable aspect of his appearance was his neck had seemingly been stretched to at least a foot in length. Wrapped around the entirety of this obscenity was what looked like an old tribal style of necklace. Lucy stared and realised the span of the decoration was made entirely out of teeth of all shapes and sizes. Rows and rows of them, discoloured by age. Lucy's mind went back to the mouths of Boudica and Dubhthach with a feeling like her mind was about to snap.

"This is my temple," the tall man smiled. "The Temple of Brennus."

Lucy silently watched Brennus hold his hands out to this underworld tomb as though it were a great source of pride for him.

"You will sustain us, or you can be extinguished immediately," he continued before taking a step forward.

Lucy noticed a curved dagger had seemingly appeared out of nowhere into the hands of the speaker.

"The choice is yours," Brennus said with a lick of his throbbing gums.

Three

Chaotic, dark corridors led Jamie closer to the source of the scream. Even though his energy levels were slowly returning, the journey was still slow going. This was in part due to him stopping to marvel at the sights unfurling before his eyes. At times he felt he could see the shadows recede to reveal the hotel corridor he had expected to find when he had escaped his room. However, each time he tried to focus on a particular section, the shadows moved and presented the ancient stone once more. His peripheral vision picked up the green glow of a fire exit sign, but as soon as he shifted his eyes to it, the shape dissolved into a mounted torch. The flame of it crackled as he passed below it.

"I'm dreaming," Jamie murmured as he continued down the corridor.

He could hear the rumbling voice of a man emanating from the direction the woman's scream had come from. Jamie grimaced and pressed on in search of answers to the disturbing puzzle he found himself trapped in.

***

Anger had galvanised Lucy from the fear and sickness. She thought of her Father's quick temper for all except her and thanked him for the gift. This fleeting memory of her superhero with the gentle smile produced a single tear that escaped the corner of her right eye and made a break for her jaw. Brennus watched the journey like a cat watching a butterfly. Lucy noted the distorted smile break over the man's large face.

"I'm not scared," Lucy thought. *"Take a step closer and find out."*

Brennus quickly turned his head towards the shadowy doorway as though alerted to something. The silence prickled before he directed Dubhthach with a click of his tongue and a tilt of his head. Lucy watched the greasy looking man disappear out of the room then cast a hateful glare towards the ancient Boudica. The old hag was almost invisible in the shadows as though she were swimming in the darkness, but Lucy could tell there was a grin lingering beneath. Brennus had turned to place the dagger on a shelf where a cluster of candles burned. Lucy wanted to make him pay for his overconfidence, but she knew playing possum while her strength returned was the best play for now.

"I suppose your mind races, child," Brennus said without turning.

He held his large hand closely above

the candles flames in an attempt to feel something, anything. Lucy watched him in silence, further enraged by being referred to as a child. Brennus turned and smirked his thick lips at her as though he had read her thoughts.

"You're a child to *me*," he held out his arms.

Lucy stared back in response and the giant of a man continued.

"I am as old as the bones of the Earth, little one. I've been here since the start, and even though my enemies trapped me in a place where my wanderings would cease, I have outlasted them all. Or so the worms tell me."

Brennus took a step closer with eyes shimmering with emotion.

"How is it fair that They can imprison my clan and I because we chose a different path? What gives them the right to look down on us?"

"Who are you?" Lucy asked through the drought in her mouth.

Brennus leaned his large skull closer to the concrete slab.

"Oh, I think you know," he cooed.

Lucy felt her anger get drenched in the icy rain of absolute terror. Brennus straightened up and returned to his rant.

"We toiled in darkness to create a gateway. Many lifetimes of digging, chanting, and suffering. Then a little light was built above us. One which we could easily manipulate."

"The hotel?" Lucy croaked.

Brennus shrugged as though he couldn't be less interested in Lucy's words.

"I care not for what it was, but for what it is now," he sneered.

Brennus walked to the nearest stone wall and traced strange patterns with one long finger. Lucy watched aghast as the familiar wall of her hotel room appeared briefly in its place. Small sparks fizzed in the lines of the tall man's drawing. Then Brennus clapped his hands once, causing Lucy to flinch, and the hotel wall was replaced with a cold stone once more.

"As you can see, this is not a hotel. It is The Temple of Brennus where we give thanks to the dark that preserves us and quenches our inner thirst."

Lucy shuddered and Brennus bared his busy gums as he walked towards her bare legs.

There was a sudden commotion in the doorway and Dubhthach fell into the room while clutching a badly broken nose. Lucy watched in shock as a man wearing only his underwear staggered into view and landed a barefooted push kick to Dubhthach's back so that the gaunt man toppled onto the hands which were still holding his nose together. Boudica screamed a horrific howl and jumped onto the back of Dubhthach's attacker. The man staggered back and sandwiched the old woman between his bare back and the stone wall. She immediately began to try and close her mouth around his neck but couldn't get the angle right.

"Hold him!" Brennus roared.

Dubhthach raised up, turned, and was instantly kicked again. This time the blow caught him under his jaw. The sound was like two Rams colliding and Dubhthach cried a distorted scream which moved some of the shadows in the room. The man with Boudica stuck to his back was wrestling with the woman but couldn't remove her. Brennus took giant strides forward and grabbed the man by his throat using just one of his huge hands. Lucy watched in amazement as he picked the man up with the old woman still attached. The man gargled and his eyes darted momentarily towards Lucy, before returning to the giant face of death before him. Lucy swung her aching legs off the slab and fought off a feeling of vertigo as she headed for the dagger.

Jamie could see black spots in every corner of his vision, and he felt the suction of the old woman's mouth finally find its target at the base of his neck. He gurgled under the immense pressure the giant of a man was placing on his throat, and he knew he didn't have long left. Without warning the man released him and Jamie fell onto his front painfully, the weight of the old woman adding to his misery. Brennus fell to one knee and gave out a cry that shook the very fabric of the room's reality. It flicked from a tomb to a hotel room and back again rapidly as though operated by a switch. Lucy took a few steps back from the dagger she had stuck between the huge man's shoulder blades and watched the brightness of the room increase. Patches of carpet grew over the stone near her feet and the hotel desk she remembered appeared to her left.

Brennus roared like a wild beast as he attempted to grab at the dagger's handle, and the room darkened once more. Jamie rolled to his feet and staggered around with Boudica still hanging on like an oversized Tick. Lucy darted forward, aimed a punch at where she thought Boudica's kidney should be and then grabbed two handfuls of long white hair. Brennus remained on his knee but watched Lucy with glowering eyes filled with hateful rage. Lucy held the giant's stare and then yanked at the white hair as forcefully as she could manage. Boudica hissed as she fell harshly onto the floor with a thump.

"Let's go!" Jamie shouted before taking off.

Lucy dodged past Boudica's flailing arms and followed Jamie out of the room.

"What the hell's going on?" she screamed after him.

Jamie reduced his speed to a jog to let Lucy close the gap.

"How the Hell should I know?"

Lucy pointed towards the lines of old

iron doors where hotel doorways should have been, but Jamie shook his head quickly.

"No good." he called out. "More of those *things*."

Right on cue a shriek shuddered up the tunnel towards them. Both Jamie and Lucy looked behind them to see Brennus and Boudica were chasing them. The shadows twisted around them and for a moment Jamie thought the old lady had grown eight legs but then they veered around a corner slightly and the view was lost.

"There was a fire exit!" he shouted to Lucy who was sprinting ahead now. "Head for that!"

Lucy responded by increasing her speed slightly and Jamie struggled to stop the gap between them from growing. Worse still he could hear the heavy feet behind him gaining ground. Jamie dared not to look so instead focused on lifting his knees up in an attempt to increase his speed. Lucy disappeared around another slight bend in the tunnel just as nearby doors creaked open as Jamie passed them. This development gave him the extra bit of pace he needed to get further away from his pursuers. Lucy came into view, and she had stopped running. Instead, she stood with her hands on her hips as she huffed oxygen into her burning lungs. Jamie was about to scream at her for stopping when he saw the dead end that lay in wait. Where there should have been a door for a fire exit there was nothing but stone.

"No," was all he could groan as he stopped at Lucy's side.

Lucy walked to the stone wall and looked back at Jamie in desperation. The sound of a dozen more iron doors slamming shut flew towards them.

"I can't let them take me," Lucy whispered.

Jamie looked at the way the twenty-something had planted her feet and clenched her fists.

"Yeah, I know," he replied softly.

A crowd of people came into view and Lucy could see Brennus looming large over all of them. Their numbers filled the width of the corridor and Jamie recoiled at the rows and rows of pulsating gums on display. Brennus pointed a huge arm over the top of his followers' heads.

"Bring them back to me," he ordered.

The mass of men and women of all ages pressed forward in response; Jamie and Lucy chanced a look at each other. Jamie nodded grimly and raised his fists in an attempt to show he was willing to fight, and Lucy nodded once in return. The murmuring from black mouths was enough to make the pair want to break out running again, but there was nowhere to go. Instead, Jamie lashed out blindly with kicks to whoever got close, and for a short while it worked. The numbers game worked against him though and one misplaced kick was met with hands that grabbed and pulled at him. Lucy waded in and hit one of the attackers across the jaw with her forearm before cleanly elbowing her next victim. A man in his fifties dropped to the floor and was swallowed up by the next bunch of the Brennus clan. Jamie was galvanised by Lucy's fighting display and promptly headbutted a young man who had tight hold of him. The pale man sagged against him, and Jamie felt totally off balance as though his feet were being taken from the ground.

"Take them!" Brennus shouted.

Jamie looked up to see the stretched man parting some of the crowd to get closer. Lucy was fighting for her life, but the weight of numbers was pushing her back, so she was only a few feet from the wall which was blocking their path. She dodged two attackers and had a quick look for Jamie. He was becoming overwhelmed by the large group and at times Lucy lost sight of him all together, but then he would rise up again like a lost sailor being moved about on a rolling ocean. Brennus ignored Jamie and waded through the sea of flesh without taking his eyes off Lucy.

"Hold her!" he boomed at those closest to his prize.

Lucy fought with everything and even took a bite at a hand that got too close.

However, deep down she knew it wouldn't be enough. Brennus was coming for her, and her legs nearly betrayed her at the thought.

Then two things happened at once. Jamie broke free and ran at Brennus as Lucy was pushed towards the wall. As Lucy lost her balance and fell backwards, she saw Jamie slam his hand into the dagger she had put into Brennus' back. Lucy heard the beginning of Brennus' scream, saw the hotel corridor resume its existence, and then it all went black. Jamie watched Lucy disappear through the stone wall as though she were a ghost and felt the faint ripple of hope in his chest. He tried to make a break for it but was jostled, until hands finally secured every limb he possessed. Hope faded as he watched Brennus compose himself and approached him slowly. The giant clamped his paw like hands around Jamie's face so they framed it completely. Brennus said nothing as he opened his mouth and leaned in. Jamie whimpered at the giant black segments as they came closer and closer until all he could see was darkness.

Four

Alan waited impatiently for the night porter to look up from his book. An old-style bell sat on the counter and Alan contemplated whether to ring it or throw it at the scruffy man in the chair.

"No wonder he doesn't work during the day," Alan thought as he appraised the untucked shirt and long, greasy hair.

"Yes?" the reader yawned at him.

"My brother was staying in room 396 and I was supposed to meet him here earlier, but I got delayed."

The night porter looked back with total disinterest and Alan couldn't stop the temper entering his throat.

"He's not answering the phone and I found out he didn't attend the last day of the conference, so?"

"So?" the greasy man wondered.

Alan slapped his hand on the marble counter and let the sting stop him from punching the man.

"So I'm trying to see if he's, ok?" he yelled.

The night porter returned his book to the drawer at his side and looked up at Alan.

"There is no room 396 in this hotel, Sir." he smiled. "Is it possible that there's been a mix up somewhere?"

"Mix up?" Alan blurted out, astounded.

Then he looked over the night porter's padded shoulder.

"I'll take the stairs." he said before setting off.

"Excuse me, Sir!" the night porter

called out.

Alan froze as he was caught in two minds. He wanted to check on his brother, but he didn't want to get in any trouble.

"That whole floor is being refurbished," the porter announced as he stood up and stretched.

When he saw Alan wasn't backing down, he shrugged dramatically.

"Ok Sir, have it your way. I'll show you."

"Ok good," Alan said, feeling as though he was making a fool of himself.

The night porter passed Alan and pressed a button on the wall.

"Let's take the elevator, Sir."

Alan nodded, and after a short wait he stepped into the cubicle with the night porter. The light flickered slightly as the elevator ascended; the night porter wondered if he should have brought the pistol he kept under the counter. After watching the mirror which displayed the thin man in his early fifties, the night porter decided with a smile he would be just fine without.

***

Alan awoke atop a hotel bed in complete darkness.

What the hell? he thought with a racing mind.

When he tried to move, he found he

didn't have the energy for the task. There was a wetness attached to his bare legs. The sound of slurping and sucking came from down there. Alan felt the life being drained from him and had a feeling he would be seeing his brother very soon.

***

The night porter pulled up his fly and moved to the large mirror that was bolted above the ground floor restroom. He looked at his reflection, sighed, and adjusted the false teeth that were so uncomfortable against his pulsating, black gums. The greasy man gave a smirk to his reflection at the thought of the angry man's demands. He left the restroom to resume his wait at the front desk. Once back he sat in his chair which let out a loud creak. He was just about to reach into the drawer for his book when he heard the safety being removed from a gun. The greasy man swung around to see a woman in a bloodied nightgown pointing his own pistol right at his face.

"Suck on *this*, you piece of shit!" Lucy roared as she squeezed the trigger.

NOTES

This is the only story I regret submitting and the reason for that is because I

65

had to pay for the honour. A rookie mistake which I won't be repeating. The positive outcome is I wrote a creepy story inspired by my teenage love of all things Clive Barker. It was an opportunity to write something I would have enjoyed reading when I first got into buying horror books. I like the concept of other worlds/dimensions being within reach so something might reach out and grab you. It allows for a nightmarish concept which I played on with the hotel/temple scenario. Leech has been around since early 2021 and I've waited and waited for a suitable call. Alas it wasn't to be, but I feel it lends strength, and straight up horror, to this collection.

Night Swimming with Mickey

The McCormick Series 5, or Mickey for short, had malfunctioned three and half hours earlier. A large piece of space debris had hit the ship and torn one of the housing plates from the magnets main mast. Bill Coffee, the only human onboard grumbled into his headset.

"How the hell am I expected to pay off the loan when I have nobody to operate the magnet?"

"Can't you repair the Mickey?" the radio asked from back on the planet Bill was orbiting.

"No, I told you!" Bill was beyond frustrated. "It's not damaged in that way; it's just acting weird."

"If it got magnetised for even a split second then the circuitry would be jacked."

Bill looked at the tubular figure currently standing in the corner. It faced the other way as though scared.

"Yeah, that's what I was thinking," he replied with a scratch of his stubble. "Look, man, I gotta go. I could have hit the quota no problem if it weren't for this, tell them that."

"You know how that will go, Bill."

"Just tell them, ok?"

"Ok. See you back here tomorrow night?"

"Yeah, see you!"

Bill threw his headset off as though it were throttling him.

"Mickey, come here."

The robot made a series of noises and Bill was reminded of a childhood visit to a mobile phone exhibition he'd seen at the museum. It was one of the only memories he had of his father, and it added to his growing sense of frustration.

"Sorry," the robot finally groaned.

Bill walked over and stood two feet taller than Mickey. The design was to help humans regain the sense of superiority when robots were performing tasks at ten time their rate of speed and competence. The robot hesitantly turned, and Bill looked at the dim lights programmed to create a friendly face.

"Can we fix you, Mickey?"

"No."

"Why the hell not?" Bill lost his temper and stamped his boot onto the steel plated floor.

"Bugs."

"It can't be a bug, Mickey. I ran diagnostics and you've had two further scans. You do not have a bug!"

There was a sudden sound like a high-pressure creak of a hull struggling under enormous pressure. Bill reacted by looking at all four corners of the deck as quickly as his eyes would allow. The sound suddenly ceased, and he turned to look at Mickey.

"Bugs," the robot confirmed.

Another sound now like the scraping of something sharp underneath them somewhere in the guts of the ship.

"What kind of bugs, Mickey?"

"Blattodea variety bug. First discovered on Erias 4."

"Blattodea?"

"Local dialect is largely unknown, but it roughly translates as metal termites."

Bill's heart sank as more damaging sounds came from below.

"Well, how the hell did they get on the ship?"

"An egg."

"Mickey, I'm beginning to think you're having fun at my expense."

"Cannot compute."

"Ok, tell me about the egg," Bill sighed wearily.

"Termite egg hit ship. Now metal termites on ship."

There was a large crash from the next room and the Robot rushed back to the corner to face the wall.

"Are you scared?"

"Cannot compute."

"Mickey?" Bill coaxed.

"Yes. They will devour my base materials in seconds. It is unsatisfactory."

Bill marched over to his chair and retrieved his bolt-gun. As he walked past Mickey, he pulled the barrel back on the weapon, so it produced a satisfying hiss.

"Well, we can't have that now can we, buddy."

"Buddy?"

Bill didn't reply as he was already through the door that led to a small area which contained his bunk, food and drink supplies, and a small table. An alarm began to sound behind Bill alerting him to the fact the hull had been breached.

"Pressure drop warning. Seventy-five percent," his ship stated.

The bravado drained from Bill at the massive initial loss. He threw his gun on the table and quickly unrolled his spacesuit. The alien synthetic shaped to his body immediately and he pulled on the helmet from under his bunk. A pleasing melody told him it was secured, and his vitals lit up on his display to remind him he was scared enough to flirt with a heart attack. Bill sealed the airlock to the storage area and marched back to the cockpit.

"I am concerned," the robot's voice called from the built-in speakers in the suits helmet.

"I sent a distress beacon out ten minutes ago and I've rerouted all power to this room."

"Metal Termites can eat through a spacecraft of this size in fifteen minutes," Mickey added.

"Well, that is not good news, I gotta tell you, Mickey."

"It is not."

Metal carnage vibrated through Bill's boots and both man and robot looked at the floor.

"This is Captain Granger of Viking 3," the radio gurgled.

Bill tapped the remote on his wrist.

"Yes, I hear you!" he shouted. "Have you locked onto our position?"

"Well yes, of course," the reply was stuffy.

"How long until you arrive?

"ETA seven minutes."

"Oh, ok." Bill panicked. "Well, we will be in the general area of the ship's last known position."

"Sorry? I don't follow."

"My ship is breaking up and I'll probably be night swimming by the time you get here."

The silence on the radio was interrupted by a scraping sound below.

"Just promise you'll look for me."

"I will." Captain Granger said quietly. *"See you soon."*

Bill grabbed the harness that he used to connect Mickey to the crane.

"Ever been in space?" Bill asked Mickey as he threw the harness on him.

"No."

"It's a lot of fun until it kills you," Bill chuckled nervously as he fastened the second part of the harness around his own waist.

The lights of the robot's display indicated it was looking at the harness which now connected them.

"This is not a good plan," Mickey said in a flat tone.

"Cabin pressure failure. Levels at 40%" the ship interrupted.

Bill checked the oxygen levels on his wrist display.

"No, it's a terrible plan," Bill squirmed in his side of the harness. "But it's the only one we have."

"We could hide?" the robot wondered.

"Wow, these bugs really have you messed-"

The floor suddenly opened beneath them, and they both fell as one before being sucked out of a larger hole into space. Bill looked back at the mass of wriggling worm-like creatures who were consuming his ship rapidly. They writhed over each other and shivered in enjoyment at the expensive materials they dined on. Diamond-like scales were embedded in the depths of their segments, and they twinkled like stars. There was something beautiful about the pure destruction of it all.

"Well, I didn't think they'd look like *that!*" he said, mainly to himself.

The pair rotated slowly away from the carnage and Bill swallowed dryly as he looked for any sign of the rescue ship.

"What does buddy mean?" Mickey asked after a few dozen rotations.

"What?"

"Earlier you referred to me as buddy. What does it mean?"

"Friend," Bill told the robot. "It means you're my friend."

"Oh."

"Is that ok with you?" Bill asked.

"My projections calculate it to be the only positive thing to have happened today," Mickey confirmed.

Bill caught a glimpse of the rapidly depleting remains of his ship.

"You're not wrong there, Mickey."

Bill looked down at the heavily polluted and ruinous planet of his birth.

"The dry ocean," Mickey pointed out.

Bill craned his neck.

"Oh, so it is."

"My data suggests you were born ninety-three years too late to swim in it."

Bill looked at the robot and enjoyed the weightless dance they performed.

"We're swimming right now, my friend. We're swimming right now."

NOTES

I LOVE the sci-fi genre. It is so compatible with horror that of course it has influenced a lot of my work to date. However, this was the first piece of sci-fi I ever wrote. I'm currently writing a sci-fi novella, and this short story was an important steppingstone to give me the confidence I needed. I like the idea of old concepts still being prevalent during a faraway future and that's what we have with this short. A hybrid of old and new technology always works for me. Our main characters are essentially mining outer space which is an environment that also doubles as an exploration of loneliness. I like the idea that a crisis could force a human and a robot to consider friendship. Our MC is a tough man who is down on his luck, but even he sees the value of such things. Especially when the cold void of outer space is one step away.

There's a sweetness to the interactions within the story and I felt quite moved while writing it. I suppose Mickey is almost like an imaginary friend we may have liked to lean on once or twice and the vulnerability and uncertainty is something we have all felt throughout our lives. Obviously, the style isn't something my usual readers will be used to, but these are always the stories I feel most proud of for that very reason. It's nice to push our boundaries of creativity.

The Pied Piper of Hamlintown

The mustard looked like something obscene on the white makeup the clown was caked in. Charlotte wrinkled her nose at the long tongue which attempted to erase the yellow smear. Her mom's warm hand touched the back of her dungarees, and even at the age of five.

Charlotte knew the gesture meant to sit back down and stop gawking.

"It's rude to stare, honey," her mom said without taking her eyes from her lunch.

"I wasn't!"

Her Dad sat opposite in the booth and held two glasses up to his eyes as though they were binoculars.

"I was."

Both mother and daughter giggled at the sight before the man, and real clown, in their lives leaned forward conspiratorially.

"It's not every day you see a clown and a strongman in the diner," he whispered with a grin.

Jennifer casually looked over her shoulder before returning to her fries.

"He's not a strongman."

Dan and Charlotte craned their necks to get a better look at the man sitting across from the burger-munching clown.

"No? What is he supposed to be then?"

"Human cannonball, and now you're both staring."

Father and daughter flushed red and lowered back down into their booth.

"Are you excited for the circus?" Dan asked and performed a drumroll with his fingers on the table.

Charlotte nodded enthusiastically before frowning and folding her arms dramatically.

"Why can't you come with us, daddy?"

Dan felt the guilt in the pit of his stomach and spewed out a default answer.

"Daddy's gotta work, sweetie."

Jennifer read the situation with her usual highspeed. She hugged her daughter into her side suddenly and kissed her brown curls.

"Daddy has to babysit the museum while we eat so much candy, we barf all over the clown's shoes."

Charlotte giggled loudly and Dan smiled politely at the two circus men who glanced over.

***

Dan locked himself behind the large, glass museum doors and raised a hand to wish the fleeing staff goodbye. Seemed like everyone was in a rush to get to the one and only show from the travelling circus. Hamlintown was small enough that it was possible everyone could be attending the show. Dan thought of Charlotte and got the familiar tightening in his gut. A sensation of love so strong he hated letting her down even if it couldn't be helped. The security job was the only one on offer to him after leaving the army on a general discharge. Dan shook the feeling away and moved from the doors in search of his coffee cup.

An hour later, he was doing his rounds when he spotted something gleaming on the floor near the stairs. Dan reached down and picked up the pretty earring. He turned it over in front of his flashlight. A strangled sound reached him. It was something calling him and singing to him at the same time. A sound so familiar yet like nothing he could recall hearing before pulled at him. In a trance, Dan dropped the earring and moved forward. His heel caught on the top step and his world suddenly pitched forward.

*⁣**

There was dry blood on his hand when he checked it. To Dan's absolute horror, the early morning light was creeping its way towards the museum entrance.

How long have I been out? Jennifer is going to kill me.

Dan checked his phone and was surprised to have received no messages from his wife. The time was 7:06 and he was pissed because he'd worked overtime for nothing: his head hurt like crazy. Had Eddie not turned up for his shift? Surely the old man would have seen him lying unconscious on the floor. Still rubbing his head, Dan retrieved his jacket, and left the museum. After locking the door, he slowly turned and winced at the morning sun. He looked up and down the street and paused. Dan expected to see the usual delivery vans, early risers, and dog walkers, but the town road was deserted. A gentle breeze passed through and although the morning wasn't cool, Dan shivered and pulled his jacket closed. He wandered to the sidewalk looking left and right. Silence was his only company, and on catching his pale reflection in the shop window opposite, he self-consciously began the short walk home.

Dan tried phoning Jennifer as a plane moved soundlessly through the clouds above him. The call went straight to voicemail, so he disconnected. The silence which followed was disturbed as a dog growled from an alleyway. Dan flinched, but when the dog immediately cowered, he slowly moved towards it.

"Hey, it's ok."

The dog took off running and Dan

frowned at the sight of the long lead dragging behind it like a useless appendage. Not one person walked by, and no vehicles passed him. By the time Dan emerged onto the street where he lived, he was running with his heart thundering in his ears. Something was very wrong and as always, his first thoughts were to protect his family. Their car wasn't in the drive, but worst of all their front door was wide open. Dan wanted to drop to his knees right there and then. Instead, he took a deep breath and ran into the house.

"Jennifer? Jen, you there?"

Silence. He noticed two half eaten meals sitting on the table. A lazy fly circling like something obscene. Dan ran up the stairs, two at a time.

"Jen? Charlotte, baby?"

The quiet seemed to mock him this time. Dan looked at the beds which were still made from the previous day. Nausea raced through him, and he closed his eyes to the panic. The house seemed alien without them, and Dan hated that it made him afraid. He rushed to his safe, punched in his code, and retrieved his Glock 19.

Dan stepped back outside and noticed the door to the Millers' house was wide open too. He didn't need to go and investigate to know their house would be empty.

What the hell is going on?

He put the gun in the waistband of his

uniform and carefully ran his hand over the lump on the back of his head. The dull ache jogged his memory until he was reliving the sensation of the strange music summoning him.

Is that what happened to everyone else? Is that what happened to my girls? I shouldn't have gone to work. I should have stayed with them and gone to the circus.

Dan stopped rubbing his skull.

The circus!

Just like thinking of the food which has poisoned you, Dan knew the circus was at the heart of the strange happenings which had led to his fall and emptied the streets of his hometown. He tried another phone call, but this time to the Sheriff's office. Dan disconnected the call when he was sure nobody was going to answer. He set off jogging for the park with a gun at his hip and a stone in his heart.

***

Dan saw the plume of smoke rising to greet the morning haze and knew it was coming from the park. His legs felt heavy as he tried to pick up the pace. The names of his loved ones caught in his throat and threatened to choke him. It was now after eight in the morning and still he'd not seen a soul. Even the birdsong seemed muted. By the time he reached Cooper Street he was a mess but had a clear view of the park. A heavily faded big top was surrounded by a network of trailers and various vehicles. The smoke was coming from behind some trees to the left of the circus and Dan jogged towards it. His military training told him to keep low from unseen threats and he entered the treeline in a crouch. Dan pulled his gun from his waistband, partly because it was digging into his hip, but mainly because he felt fear crackling across every nerve in his body. There was a stench in the air which Dan had encountered more than once in Afghanistan. He moved forward and the view made him collapse against the nearest tree.

Dan tried to control the sobs which wanted to escape him and waited until his stomach stopped contracting. He leaned out and observed the maddening pile of men and women stacked atop each other like scraps from an abattoir. Butchered bodies and broken bones jutted out in a sickening display. There were faces which Dan vaguely recognised and he was forced to look away. His eyes roamed to the source of the smoke where blackened corpses lay like coals in the fires of Hell. The bonfire was three times the size of the nearest pile of bodies: tears prickled and fell from Dan's eyes.

He knew in his soul that his wife was burning there.

Charlotte!

He looked back at the bodies and forced his eyes to explore. As far as he could tell, there were no children lying amongst the dead. There was slight movement from the human debris and Dan followed the twitching hand up to the Sheriff's uniform. He met Sheriff McCoy's dying eyes whose last act was to blink rapidly as a warning before indicating to the right of the fire. Dan sank down into cover just as the clown from the diner emerged with a scruffy looking man in a silk onesie. The clown in particular looked like something left out in the garbage. His costume was covered in old stains, and he loped along like something inhuman. Dan kicked himself for not realising something was off in the diner. He wondered if he could have told Jennifer not to go to the stupid circus. The men's feet come closer and moved towards the stack of bodies.

"I wish the kids would quit crying," said one.

"Shut up and lift," replied the other.

Dan's heart was galvanised with the news Charlotte could still be alive. He didn't know what evil had been unleashed on his town, but he knew he had to act right that very second.

Dan raised his gun from cover, and then checked himself. A gunshot would alert any other potential threats and his daughter could very well be a hostage. The thought of his little girl propelled him from behind the tree as though he were a mountain lion. Dan hit the clown with his shoulder and sent him flailing into the flames where he landed face down. The other man was stunned and still held the ankles of the corpse when Dan clubbed him savagely with the pistol. It was a blow which connected with the man's temple and sent him staggering around as though drunk. Dan tackled him to the ground and buried punches into his face until the only movements from below were spasm-like twitches.

A woosh sounded from the fire and when Dan looked, he felt as though his heart had become unattached. The clown stepped out of the fire and stood as though watching him. Dan slowly stood and took in the sight. The flames had melted the silk costume into the clown's bubbling flesh and all his hair was gone. Dan blinked rapidly to dislodge the sight as the clown took a shaky step forward. He feared he would have to use the gun, but the clown suddenly keeled over and lay still as smoke came away from his severely burned flesh. Small flames still worked at the clown and Dan spat towards it before moving away in search of his daughter.

The chanting began when he moved around the first empty caravan. It was a sound which changed the air and Dan found he was grinding his teeth in response. He recalled the noise which had caused him to fall at the museum. Dan wondered if the strange noise which had compelled him forward had also summoned the town to their doom. He worked his way forward in a low crouch as he negotiated the maze of trailers. Dan tried to shut off the part of his brain which was calculating how many members of the circus he might face. The chant intensified, but there was another noise which came to him on the gentle morning breeze. It was a sound which chilled him to the bone.

Children mewling like new-born kittens.
Charlotte!

Dan rushed as much as he dared until he reached the inner circle of caravans. What he saw as he peeked around the corner took his breath away. All the circus workers stood in a line, holding hands, and chanting an ancient song which Dan couldn't understand. Clowns stood next to acrobats who joined hands with strong men, a magician, and a lion tamer. The figures were all shapes and sizes with strange costumes the likes of which Dan would not associate with a modern circus. They did, however, all have one thing in common. Each man and woman were covered in the gore of the community they'd recently butchered.

Something was in the middle of the congregation and Dan craned his neck to get a better view. There was a wooden mannequin which had been dressed in what looked like a ringmaster's outfit. A top hat was placed on the varnished head while a long black cape occasionally moved with the breeze. The chanting continued and Dan's head spun with the dizzying sensation it provoked. He found it hard to look at the mannequin as though the haze of fumes were preventing his eyes from focusing. Dan blinked rapidly and swore he saw the angular face of moustachioed man.

A murmur of crying came from somewhere to the right and Dan knew the children were being held somewhere in that direction. He turned to move away to find them but changed his mind. The sick congregation, covered in the blood of his wife and their neighbours, mocked him. Dan needed to save his little girl but the compulsion for revenge clawed at him like a rat trapped in his chest. He had fifteen bullets, and he was a good shot. Yet, he hesitated. The Circus was something evil, and Dan worried bullets may not be enough.

Charlotte.

The little girl's name was enough to make up his mind. However, as Dan moved away from his hiding place, the chanting suddenly stopped. His skin crawled as he realised the congregation had turned to observe him. Twisted grins and fangs snarled under eyes which bristled with rage. The lion tamer took a step forward and Dan shot him twice in the chest without hesitation. Dust erupted from the wounds and the man cracked his whip menacingly. More figures moved around, and Dan knew they were already trying to cut off his escape. An acrobat walked on her hands towards him and emitted a throaty laugh. Dan squeezed off three more shots in an act of desperate defiance. Dust erupted from the woman, and her laugh intensified. It was a sound which was suddenly lost in her throat, and she fell to the grass in a tangle. All eyes snapped around to the mannequin and Dan saw one of his bullets had caught it. Now all the eyes of the circus were filled with fear. Dan aimed at the strange, varnished dummy.

The magician screamed an ancient word, and a fireball flew from his outstretched hands. Dan felt the heat of it as he dived out of the way. The stampede of feet came for him, and Dan rolled and blind-fired in the general direction of the shrine. He jumped to his feet and narrowly avoided the three knives a juggler had thrown at him. The magician circled to get a better sight through the crowd of attackers as Dan did the same to try and shoot the mannequin once more. All the while his mind screamed his daughter's name like a mantra.

Charlotte!
Charlotte!
Charlotte!

The strongman caught hold of Dan by the throat and lifted him up. Huge hands squeezed the life out of him as he was slammed into the nearest caravan. Dan felt the darkness coming for him but caught sight of concern on the magician's face. Then he realised, the strongman had elevated him above the crowd and foolishly given him the perfect line of sight. Dan wheezed for air as he raised the Glock. When the bullets came the noise sounded as though it were underwater. The mannequin splintered badly, and the strongman's arm collapsed in on itself and turned to ash. All fell to their knees and sobbed and begged, but Dan emptied the clip into the strange statue. The wood was shredded, and each person involved in the strange ceremony crumbled until Dan stood alone and panting for breath. He ran towards the sound of crying children.

The cage was full to the bars with kids of all ages. They cowered and flinched as Dan rushed towards them.

"Charlotte?" he yelled in a strangled voice.

The cage was secured with a padlock and Dan drew his gun.

"Everyone step back."

The children screamed as the bullet did its job. All froze in place until a familiar voice called from the huddle.

"Daddy?"

Dan broke down crying as his little girl emerged past the legs of some older children. Charlotte ran to him, and he held her as tightly as he dared. On seeing this, the other children understood Dan wasn't part of the circus and began filing out of the cage. Dan scooped his daughter up and she pressed her wet eyes to his neck. He didn't know exactly what he was going to do but he knew he had to get the children away from the bodies of their loved ones.

"Follow me. Let's get out of here."

They walked down the middle of empty streets in traumatised silence. Dan carried Charlotte at the front of the procession with the town's young following in a line behind him. He recalled a legend he'd heard in childhood and couldn't stop feeling like the Pied Piper as he led the children out of their hometown. They wept for the empty homes they left behind. Their town was filled only with the corpses of their loved ones now. Dan held Charlotte close and suppressed the sobs which wanted to leap from him. He prayed to a god who had long since abandoned him that there would be help in the next town. They passed a sign.

Thanks for visiting Hamlintown!

None in the crowd noticed the severely burnt figure stalking them through the trees which flanked the road. The clown kept pace knowing the death of the town's final adult would complete the ritual and his circus would return to tour once more.

NOTES

I was invited to a call and then the publisher disappeared leaving some quality writers (and me ((EDITORS NOTE: AND ME))) in limbo. These things happen. To some people they happen a lot. It was a no-brainer to include this here. I wrote it earlier this year after having the opening scene rattling around my head for way too long. For those that don't know me well, my education is more geared towards film making, which is to blame for my usual fast-paced narratives and action-packed set-pieces. Which is why I envisioned the opening to the story playing out like the opening to a movie. The two circus performers sitting eating burgers in a diner without an ounce of humour was something which I found striking. The little girl would, just like my little girl, kneel on her seat to get a better view and the whole thing would feel very odd. It was a scene I knew I had to use on something and I'm glad I got to use it to start this story.

Another scene which wouldn't leave me be is the closing one with the father leading the kids away from the death behind them. The title is of course based on the folklore I'm sure you're familiar with. There are some variations which see the pied piper leading the children to a paradise of sorts, but in the main it's a pretty messed up tale which you should go and revisit when you get the chance. With my story I liked the idea of our heavily defeated main character leading a mass retreat from an evil adversary.

The sting in the tail had to be the clown in pursuit because now in my tale we don't know if our hero gets to paradise or death either. Clowns are pretty off limits at times due to the success of famous horror versions, but because he was the star of the opening, mine had to feature at the end too.

The Main Road Through

The sound of late-night traffic always soothed Liam; so, no matter whether it was hot or cold, he would always sleep with his bedroom window open. He would be well into his dreams once the sounds had died away and most people were either in bed or on shift at work. However, his last couple of sleeps had been disrupted by a strange noise which had found its way into his consciousness. At first just a manipulation of his dreams, then a nagging thought at breakfast time which he could not hold onto. Finally, at 3:15a.m on Tuesday he was disturbed enough to actually hear it. He sat upright with enough force to wake his girlfriend up.

"What's up?"

The sound had gone and only the buzz of silence hung in the air like static.

"Dunno, I heard something on the road, but it sounded all wrong?"

Rach had already dozed back off.

"Like a broken van or something, but... Different," Liam murmured.

He lay back down to sleep and floated

through strange nightmare he'd forget by the morning. His sleep-self fell in slow motion towards a hooded demon at the bottom of the stairs.

"Did you not hear it at all?" Liam asked with a mouth full of toast at breakfast.

Rach was straightening her hair for work and Liam was about to repeat himself before she finally answered.

"Hear what?"

"Last night. That weird noise."

Rach spun around to shoot him a look.

"Oh yeah, you woke me up, you knob. You were tossing and turning after that. No wonder I'm tired!"

Liam walked over and put his arm around her shoulders.

"Sorry love." he said, wincing. "But did you hear it?"

"I heard you snoring, and that's weird enough."

Liam walked over to the sofa and sat to watch the latest sports news.

"I think it's been doing it all week."

Rach stood up and checked her long brown hair in the mirror.

"Going to meet Sergio?" Liam teased.

"Ha-ha. You know it's my important meeting today. Remember those?"

Liam laughed and stretched his long arms.

"Don't be bitter because I'm my own

boss."

"Then maybe turn your computer on at least?" Rach kissed him on the top of his head.

"Let me turn you on instead?"

"Jesus," Rach snorted and promptly left.

The door slammed shut and Liam was left alone in the lounge.

The news reporter spoke of race hate, Liam shook his head and switched the television off. He lifted the lid on his laptop and entered his password. Liam's mind relaxed and he found himself standing waiting for the kettle to boil; even though he couldn't recall moving from the lounge. As the water agitated, Liam began to feel pressure on his inner ear. He grabbed the worktop and knocked off a spoon but managed to steady himself. The sound of the kettle became warped, and Liam closed his eyes. Now the kettle was no longer a kettle at all. Instead, it sounded like something he only heard at 3:15am.

**

"What's the matter?" Rach asked as she put her book down on the bedside table.

Liam squirmed his legs out of the bed covers.

"Just restless, love. I feel like I just wasted the day."

Rach rolled onto her side to face him and gave him a comforting smile.

"It feels like that sometimes, doesn't it?"

"No, I mean I don't know where it went. Like I..." he searched for the words. "I was making a drink and next thing it's bedtime."

Rach frowned. Liam could feel her analysing him but was feeling too helpless to contest.

"You're taking your tablets right, babe?"

"For fucks sake, Rach."

He stood up and walked around the bed to the window.

Rach watched him as he peered through a gap in the curtains.

"Something happened today and it's not my fault. I heard that noise in the house."

"I'm not saying anything is your fault. What do you mean in the house?"

Liam returned to the bed and sat on the edge with his back to his girlfriend.

"I don't know," he rubbed his eyes. "I'm on top of my meds, Rach."

"Ok babe, I'm sorry."

A hand on his back now.

"But I'm allowed to be worried about you, you know?"

"I know, Rach. I'm going to get some water. Do you want anything?"

"No, I'm fine. I need to sleep."

Rach rolled to face the wall as Liam walked out of the bedroom.

I need sleep too, he thought.

Sleep would not come though. He lay

there with eyes wide open to the darkness of the bedroom as he tried to make sense of his day. No matter what he tried, his mind kept clouding over. The more he tried, the more frustrated he became until he eventually rolled on his side and was met with the red digits on the alarm clock.

3:15a.m.

A sound was coming up the main road his street spewed out onto. It sounded like old engineering. All diesel and vibrating metal. There was something else occurring simultaneously which he could not quite grasp. It belonged to the machine coming up the road, closer now, but it did not make sense. Somewhere between a flute and a moan. Liam looked over at Rach fearfully, but she was fast asleep. The noise grew louder and louder as it came closer and closer. His mind raced as to what it could be, so he crept out of bed to approach the window. After three steps the sound completely stopped, silence buzzed in Liam's ears like a fly with horrific secrets.

He froze with his eyes wide, while craning his neck to ensure no sound remained to give him a clue of the nightly disturbance.

Nothing.

He looked once more at Rach hoping she would anchor him to the real world, and then tread slowly to the window. Liam slowly, pulled the curtain to one side and let out a startled breath. For in the middle of the main road stood a man who looked directly back at him from some forty metres. Liam immediately felt as though he should not be looking at the man and began to release the curtain.

No, why shouldn't I look? He's staring into my bedroom, he thought, suddenly angry.

The man in the road was wearing a tattered suit which hung off him like when a child tries on their parent's clothes. His face seemed to be so incredibly pale under the streetlights, it appeared to be almost translucent. He held his arms to his sides as though waiting.

Right then, Liam thought as he made for the bedroom door.

He didn't even consider Rach as he ran noisily down the stairs to the front door.

Liam's heart thundered as he turned the key and decided it was wise to go and grab a golf club before he confronted the man. As he opened the cupboard under the stairs to retrieve a weapon of leisure, he heard the strange engine start up outside. Was it diesel or steam? Liam couldn't tell. He rushed back to the door as the sound intensified but by the time he opened it and looked out, the street was empty, and the sound was fading into the distance. The silence that followed was disturbing enough for Liam to shiver and close the door quickly.

"What the hell is going on?" Rach shouted from the top of the stairs as Liam began to feel dizzy again.

***

Liam rolled onto the piece of paper that lay beside him. He suddenly became aware he was alone in his bedroom and quickly sat up.

Did I faint?

He looked at the clock and it said 22.35.

"What?" he said to the digits.

How could that be? It must have been around half past three in the morning when he had stood at the front door.

Think. Think. The street had been empty, and he had shut the door and then. Rach?

Liam grabbed at the paper note from under him. He immediately recognised his girlfriend's writing and felt his heart sink with nausea.

Liam,

I can't take this anymore. You haven't been yourself for so long. I tried to give you time because I honestly thought that you were getting better but if anything, you're getting worse. You must be so far behind in your work that it actually scares me. In the day you refuse to talk, and you just sit around as though you're in a trance. At night you only want to talk about a noise

THAT NOBODY ELSE CAN HEAR, LIAM! You wake me up constantly moving from bed to the window and twice you've gone outside and left the front door open. I love you so much babe, but this has gone on for weeks now and I can't take it. Gone up to my Mums. Please dont too upset. If you want to do something for me then please book an urgent appointment to see Dr Patel.

Rach x

"Weeks?" Liam's heart raced.

How is that possible? What's she talking about?

He jumped out of bed and instinctively looked out of the window. Her car was gone. Liam opened the wardrobe to see empty hangers.

He started to weep.

What's happening? I don't understand.

Liam ran downstairs to look for his phone and after a time found it next to the kettle. The battery was completely dead which was unusual in itself. Liam realised he didn't even know what day it was and suddenly began to feel very unwell. He walked slowly over to the sofa and lay down on it. A numb sensation filled his mind which made it impossible to process any of his thoughts. He closed his eyes to it all.

Liam was awoken by a gentle tapping on his living room window. The sound alerted him to the spluttering engine noise that idled on the main road. He didn't bother to look at the clock. Liam knew what time it was. Instead, he sat up and walked to the front door, opened it, and stepped out into the cool air. He suddenly realised he was only wearing lounge pants, a vest, and nothing on his feet. There was of course nobody near his window. No owner of the light knocking. From where he stood the corner house on the opposite side of the street blocked out his view of the main road. He walked across the path a little so he could see the source of the peculiar engine noise.

After a few strides, the engine suddenly cut off as though it had been powered down. All that remained was a sound which froze Liam to the spot. It was a mix of sobbing, wailing, and howling. At times it seemed near and then suddenly it sounded miles away as though taken away on a strange breeze. Just when he didn't think he could take it anymore, the sound too, abruptly ceased. Liam waited a moment, scared the noise would begin anew. After a minute of his blood thundering in his ears to the beat of his ragged breathing, he decided to keep moving along the path. He walked as though dreaming to where the main road would come into view.

Liam stopped to take in what his eyes

could not believe. For before him was a sort of wagon he had never seen anything like in his life. It looked like a steam train had crashed into an HGV and they had merged together. Smoke was constantly coming up from under its low bodywork like fog which made Liam squint to gather more details. The back section appeared to be writhing as one, but every time he felt he could make something out, a fresh plume of smoke washed across the scene. A creak from the front of the vehicle startled him and he instinctively took a step backwards as legs emerged from an open door. The man in the suit jumped down into the road in a movement devoid of fluidity. Liam looked at the dishevelled suit and up to the hollowed-out eyes. Or was it shadows from the streetlight? The man had no hair at all. Not even eyebrows. It seemed like he only had a layer or two of skin stretched over his skull and this puckered when he spoke.

"It's your turn to drive." his voice seemed in Liam's ear and far away at the same time.

"What are you talking about? Who are you?"

The man took a step towards Liam and brushed dust from the front of his jacket.

"Who I am is unimportant. Only that my time is served and now it's your time."

"I don't know what you mean?"

"Again, that is not important. Please get

in and drive away."

Liam looked at the man's bony finger and then at the vehicle he pointed at. The smoke briefly cleared, and to his horror Liam realised the back of the vehicle was a sort of trailer decorated with a tangle of human beings. It was naked flesh he'd seen writhe, and they now turned their eyes to him and began wailing.

"Jesus Christ," Liam sobbed.

"No. No I don't think so," the skin mask smirked.

The man took another step forward and now pointed at the very mass which Liam couldn't take his eyes from.

"They need taking to the other place. Every night more will join them, and it will be your job to see that it happens."

Now the man was closer, Liam caught the stench of something rotting.

"What other place?" he cried, taking a few steps back.

"Oh, you know."

"No, I don't. None of this makes sense. Christ this is a bloody nightmare."

The man's demeanour suddenly changed, and he seemed to grow beneath his suit.

"It's your job now. It's your job now," he spat at him.

Liam was shaking his head violently.

"No. No. No. I'm not going anywhere

near that thing."

The man rushed him and grabbed hold of his wrist. Liam recoiled in terror at the ice like touch.

"Stay away from me you freak!" he screamed as he broke free.

Liam turned and began to run back home. The wailing from the vehicle intensified and he heard violent cries of protest. The man in the suit stood in the middle of the road and screamed.

"It's your job now! Not mine. It's your job now!"

Over, and over again.

Liam rushed into his house and locked his door. He pushed a wooden side table, so it acted as a barricade. Then he checked if all windows were shut, and if the back door was locked and suitably barricaded. By the time he was done he was sweating profusely, and the sounds outside had disappeared.

***

Liam had woken and then slept and woke again. He wasn't sure how many times he had fallen asleep, but the dizzy spells had kept him rooted to his sofa. Whenever he stood up, he would feel unsteady to the point of nausea until eventually he vomited all over the carpet. Then he just had to crash back down onto the sofa and put up with the fumes from it. In the early hours of the morning, he heard tapping at the window. Night after hellish night. Always gentle at first but then giving way to an impatient hammering. Liam imagined the bony hand on the outside of the glass and shivered to remember its touch.

Day time was not something he ever remembered now. He only seemed to be conscious during the dark hours, and even then, he felt moving was too much of a strain so instead lay there trying not to think of anything at all. It was during one of these moments he had awoken in the darkness lying in what he initially thought was more vomit, only to realise it was a pile of hair on which he had salivated. Liam brushed his hand over his head and the last of his hair fell away with the touch.

"Oh God no."

He sat up, closing his eyes to steel himself against the sudden dizziness. His world had come apart at the seams and he could not explain it. He put his hands to his face. His eyebrows were gone, and his skin felt strange, like wax. There wasn't even stubble along his jaw anymore. Liam sat in darkness as the lights had been making him feel worse. He opened his eyes and squinted at the clock on the wall. When it had become stuck on quarter past three, he could not tell. He looked at his hands which seemed somehow smaller than he remembered.

Liam heard the strange vehicle before the tapping began on his window.

"How long has it been?"

He managed to stand slowly and walked to the hallway. By the time he had struggled the wooden unit out of the way the tapping had become a loud and desperate hammering.

"Alright, alright."

Liam noticed a photo frame had become displaced by his barricade making. The picture within was of a happy couple enjoying the sunshine in a park. He felt like he knew the woman somehow, but he could not place the smiling man. With that he opened the door and stepped out into the freezing air. There was no one around so he headed towards the sound of the strange vehicle. In the road there was a crumpled suit lying in a pile. Liam picked up the jacket and put it on before walking to the door of the vehicle. He took one last look around at the buildings but did not recognise any of them. There was sad moaning from the back of the vehicle, so Liam got in and sat behind the wheel.

"Ok, ok. We're going," he called out through a puckered smile.

NOTES

This is the first short story I wrote after deciding to give writing a go in 2020. It was inspired by moving to the house I currently live in. Just like our main character, I kept being awoken by a strange sounding vehicle driving down the main road opposite my house. I never got a look at it, but it must have had a trailer with various pieces of equipment on it because the wind blowing through it made it sound so unnatural. After a few weeks it stopped passing by, but it left enough of an impression on me to really run with the idea of some strange contraption driving our roads as we all slept. It was a conscious decision not to have any major action or gore within the story because I'd just come off writing what was to become The Cursed Caves and The Cursed Creatures and there is certainly enough of that within those pages! I screwed around with the perception of time within the narrative without realising it was something which really freaks my girlfriend out. Unfortunately for her, she also happens to be my most trusted beta reader. Oops!

Nothing But Ashes

Erin,
By the time you read this, they'll already be coming for you.

The frigid air of her father's old cabin dropped a few degrees as Erin's wide eyes scanned across her ex-boyfriend's scribbled words. She'd noticed the envelope on the floor immediately and still had her large rucksack on her back. The fact Alex had been at the cabin recently, even if it were just to push a letter under the door, made Erin's mouth turn dry and sickly. Fear was rising up in giddying waves as she continued to read from the note in her shaky hand.

I know how much you love the isolation up there... Hell you certainly wanted the isolation from me! But for once it's going to work against you. Nobody fucks me over like you did, Erin. NOBODY! So now payback is going to be as big a bitch as you are. Those friends of mine you didn't like. Well, they didn't like you either. They introduced me to some truly depraved forums out in the corners of the internet. We've been having some interesting chats with some of their most perverted members. People looking to scratch an itch which normal life won't allow for. Your Daddy's cabin is the only structure for about fifty miles, and you were both proud of that, weren't you? Well, I was proud of it too. So proud that I put its coordinates into every twisted forum I could find. Not only that, but I also put a photo of you alongside them with a promise.

Erin felt tears running down her cold cheeks and sagged against the wall. A picture of her father holding up a large trout cracked between her pack and the wood.

The promise is if they provide evidence of your bloody demise, I will send them coordinates for the big bag of money I stashed. But honestly, these creatures probably don't give a shit about the cash. Being up there, away from the real world, so they can play out their sick fantasies is the real prize. Believe me when you read this, sweet Erin - they're coming for you and there is no escape. You messed with the wrong one and now you pay the price!

A sob left Erin's throat like a ricochet from her soul as she dropped the paper threat to the floor. She staggered towards the small table which faced the open door and the cracked picture frame fell unnoticed behind her. Alex had been charming and exciting, but her friends had warned of rumours of criminality and shady behaviour. He'd charmed her though, and for a while, things had been good. His perfect gentleman routine had eroded under the strain of drugs and secretive meetings. Alex had raised his hand to her once, and she'd left. Erin thought she'd been one of the lucky ones to get out at the very start. At the time, the hardest thing had been keeping her dad from retaliating. Now, as Erin threw off her rucksack and placed her palms on the table, she realised luck had never been a factor. She sucked in air and blew it through the floating dust which the lazy sunlight showed her. Her hands were tanned and hardened to a life of outdoor pursuits, and they clenched to fists at the thought of her ex-boyfriend.

In a flurry of movement, Erin marched out of the cabin with a mind full of threats and her father's teaching. Behind the cabin was around twenty metres of rocky land followed by a sheer drop of dizzying proportions. Erin secured the climbing rope and threw the other end out into oblivion. This would be her exit but first there were things to fetch from the cabin and preparations to make. She backtracked the route of her hike around tall trees until a grey outcrop came into view. With the confident strides of one who had performed the task countless times, Erin jumped up onto the rocks to look down across the valley. Dazzling light reflected off the bodywork of parked cars turned tiny by the distance. Erin squinted at the clearing and counted four vehicles. Smoke gyrated to the sky near the makeshift car park. The flames were obscured by trees, but Erin pictured grotesque men with wet smiles and sweat stained shirts warming their hands. They were in no rush and that was their first mistake.

***

David Barker was smugly striding closer to his prize when white hot agony vibrated through his shin. He toppled onto his backside and screamed at the bear trap which he'd never get to remove. David would still be lying there when the wolves visited.

Jake McColl was the only man near enough to hear the scream, but Erin moved in silence behind him. The rock opened up the back of his skull, so he was dead before his face crashed into the dirt. Erin snaked back towards the cabin with venomous thoughts of Alex coursing through her veins. She knew he was capable of bad deeds; it was why she had broken things off, but this was truly evil. He'd always been controlling, and she'd lost good friends because of it.

Erin put her hand to the keys in her pocket and thought of her father. She could use his help, but at the same time, she was happy he was too old to visit the cabin. If anything were to happen to him because of a psycho ex, she'd never forgive herself.

The cabin was no longer a sanctuary,

the same way her father was no longer stalking deer through the forest. Erin let out a ragged breath at the thought of her dad. The toughest, sweetest man she knew, who couldn't get up the mountain because his arthritis was crippling him. One moment he was carrying her for miles on his shoulders, the next he was looking up helplessly from the armchair he needed help getting up from.

"Hey, sugar,"

A leering voice broke the memory to pieces and Erin cursed herself for getting distracted. Arms held her tight from behind as a man pressed himself against her rear.

"You're all mine now, baby," the boozy warm voice said into her neck.

Erin looked down at a worn tennis shoe. It was ridiculously out of place on the mountain and a further reminder of how ill prepared these men were. Erin stomped her heavy boot down and threw her head back simultaneously. The arms released her with a yelp and Erin turned to get a good look at her latest attacker. His glasses were broken along with his nose, and Erin sneered at the man's pasty skin and lank comb-over. He was bleeding over a hooded sweater which had an image of Mariah Carey on it. The man was about to curse Erin out, but the point of her lock knife burst his eyeball. A wet pop exploded in his head as the eye mashed into brain, and his legs fell from under him. Erin

111

spat on the man and hurried away through the trees in the direction of the smaller store cabin.

Thankfully, the storage unit was well camouflaged, so there were no signs it had been tampered with. Erin unlocked the door which opened with a sharp creak. Inside was a well-insulated lockbox so Erin fumbled with another smaller key. Her eyes fell to the satellite phone, and she smirked against the bitter rage. After self-consciously checking over her shoulder, she removed the items needed to defend herself. The weight of the mountaineering axe was a welcome sensation. Erin's father had been judged unfairly at times due to his survivalist outlook. Many people saw it as an unhealthy mindset especially when he would disappear into the mountains for weeks on end with his young daughter.

"What about her schooling?" they'd complain.

"Erin is getting the education she really needs, don't you worry about that," her dad would reply.

What many didn't consider was it was something the man had leaned into when his wife had died. Erin had been young, but she'd understood more than anyone that it was better for her dad to be hauling tinned goods out to a hidden cabin than staring at old photographs like a zombie. She was lucky to have so many memories with the man. Fortunate to see the smile back on his face while they roamed the woods and hills.

Erin's dad had been teaching her for an extinction level event. She couldn't believe it would be a personal vendetta against her which would test all the training. As Erin took up position in a dense tree, she recalled the day she surprised her dad by arriving at the cabin with Alex. She remembered the hurt in her father's eyes. At the time she thought it was because he was somehow wounded by having another man there with her grownup daughter, but now she saw it for what it was. Her dad had been disappointed because despite the years of teachings, his daughter had brought a stranger into their secret inner sanctum. It was a move which jeopardised the whole point of having a place to escape to when the world went to shit. Erin ruefully considered just how wrong things had gone. Surely even her ultra-prepared dad couldn't have imagined her current situation. "I'm gonna clean this up, dad," Erin murmured to steel herself.

***

Jason and Jacob were identical twins. They'd always revelled in the awkwardness presented to them when other people fumbled around their identity. As kids they had played pranks on their parents by pretending to be each other, and when that stopped getting a reaction, they pretended to forget which one

113

they were until their mother would cry with the torment of it. Then, as teens, they realised pretending to be one entity, and sharing a life was where the real fun lay. Sometimes they would get bored of a relationship and just swap. The real excitement came from revealing their tricks to partners after months, sometimes years. It was hard to remember how many people they'd messed up with their games, but it was a lot. As the years passed, their tastes became more perverse until they spent all their free time in the shadows of the dark web. Jacob looked across at Jason as they ambled up the hill. It was still a thrill to see a living replica of himself. Today they wore black combat pants tucked into boots. Jason looked back at Jacob and admired the black trench coat they were both wearing. Their long black hair was tied back into tight ponytails, and they wore the same satisfied look of hunters.

An impact sound disrupted the calm and sent creatures skittering in all directions. It reminded Jacob of the noise when they had thrown axes into the wooden target in the trendy bar from last weekend. Jason had fallen a few steps behind and when Jacob turned to check on him his guts froze. His twin was looking down at his feet while a newly disrupted strand of hair dangled down towards a blood-spattered rock. Jason made a strange wheezing cough and looked up with eyes full of terror. Jacob gasped at the crossbow bolt which had impaled his brother's chest. Jason coughed a mouthful of blood into his brother's face and keeled over. Jacob reeled from the gore and wiped it from his eyes just in time to receive a crossbow bolt there. He thought he could hear running water right up until his legs gave out. The fall knocked the bolt out through the back of his skull. Erin tossed the crossbow to the foot of the tree and then climbed down. No more bolts remained, so she left the weapon behind with the dead twins.

Erin's instinct sent her snaking back down the track once more until she was at the large outcrop of rocks. To her horror, half a dozen more vehicles had joined the ones she'd seen earlier. In fact, the valley looked more like the parking area for a music festival than the field she was used to seeing. There was no way she could deal with such superior numbers. It was time to make her escape. Erin turned straight into a punch which sent her skidding on her backside. She looked up to see a large man wearing tactical gear and a balaclava.

Erin rubbed the pins and needle from her cheek as the masked man enjoyed standing over her. His victim swiftly pulled a flare gun from her waistband and pointed it at his face with a smirk. The man's eyes grew wide, and he was about to plead, when the trigger was pulled. Erin squinted as the round embedded itself in her attacker's face and began to spark and smoke. The man dropped to his knees and tried to take his mask off, but the flare was melting through his nose cartilage like white-hot plasma. Erin looked away as he pulled at the mask with both hands. Skin peeled from his cheeks and the man fell down with his face still melting inwards as a plume of smoke snaked to the treetops.

Erin set off running back towards the cabin. She cursed Alex for being so viciously vindictive. As she swatted branches out of the way, Erin wondered what motivated him to be so evil. Alex was a control freak who wasn't used to people saying no to him. The thought of her ex-boyfriends controlling nature stopped Erin in her tracks. Alex had hand delivered the letter.

He'd want to be here, her mind raced. *He's still here.*

Erin shivered and closed her eyes to the dizzying cocktail of fear and rage. She set off running faster than before and was soon back at the cabin where all appeared tranquil. Erin locked the door to the smell of petrol. The liquid seeped underneath and followed her outside. She thanked her dad for owning the backup generator and threw the handful of lit matches into the emerging puddle. The flames grew higher as Erin rushed around the back of the cabin with her newly acquired mountaineering gear. Fire licked the rear of the cabin now. Smoke was seeping through every gap in the cabin by the time Alex started screaming and throwing himself against the door. He'd smashed the bedroom window, but it was too small for his escape.

The wailing reached a terrifying pitch before the door buckled under Alex's' assault. A shrieking fireball was all that was left of the man, but he still rushed towards Erin for his revenge. Each stride created a terrible whoosh of fanned flames which refused to go out. Erin held her ground until the last moment to make sure Alex was fully committed to reaching her. She saw his pained eyes in the flames, flipped him the bird, and dropped out of sight with the guide rope fastened to her belt. The fire passed overhead, and she watched it flapping by like a flightless bird. Alex wailed like a baby all the way to the rocks below. Erin began her descent and looked forward to seeing her ex-boyfriend one last time. Those who remained on the mountain would find nothing but ashes, and maybe a bear trap or two.

***

It was dark and Steve and Tony sat opposite each other staring at the phone. Bill had been so agitated he'd gone to have a lie down upstairs, while Chad went out for supplies over an hour ago. They had all stressed and argued over the same topic all evening. Alex should have been in contact by now. Something had gone wrong. Bill had tried to argue Alex was just playing it cool, but they all knew he would have been in touch by now to gloat about Erin's death.

"Maybe the police picked him up," Tony said to the quiet lounge.

Steve thought about it for a moment and then just shook his head.

"You got any better ideas?" Tony snapped.

The flashpoint came to nothing as the men had already suffered hours of tension and animosity. There was a confident knock at the front door and both men couldn't hide their smiles as relief fell away and their shoulders relaxed. Steve marched to the door before checking himself and holding out his hand to Tony.

"Pass me the piece."

Tony seemed perplexed at his friend's paranoia but passed over the Glock they shared. Steve looked through the peephole and quickly addressed Tony over his shoulder.

"It's Chad," he whispered.

Tony was disappointed as he'd hoped it had been Alex returning.

"Let him in then."

Steve returned to the peephole.

"He looks messed up."

Tony barged Steve away from the door to take a look. Indeed Chad appeared to be swaying and his head was slumped over as though he were drunk. Tony opened the door in a hurry and Chad fell into his arms. The immediate warmth on his arms told him Chad was bleeding copiously.

"Fuck!"

Steve held the gun to the outside world and scanned from side to side. Once satisfied there was nobody hiding out there, he slammed the door and locked it again.

"Jesus, Chad stay with me, man," Tony whimpered.

Steve looked down at Chad bleeding out in Tony's arms. His friend looked like he was made of tissue paper and the amount of blood on the floor made him feel dizzy.

"I'll get some towels," he mumbled as he staggered from the room.

Steve entered the kitchen and froze. The back door was moving slowly in the breeze, and he held the gun to it in a shaky hand. Finally he took a few hesitant steps forward just as the wind caused it to slam shut. Steve moved the bolt across quickly as the hairs on his neck stood on end.

Chad shuddered in Tony's arms and died. Steve ran into the lounge and Tony looked up with a tear-streaked face.

"The backdoor was open," Steve hissed.

Tony was about to breakdown about Chad's death when there was a thumping sound from the staircase at the back of the room. Both men turned as a blur fell down the steps. Only when it rolled off the bottom step and onto the lounge carpet did they realise the object was Bill's severed head.

Steve whipped the gun up to aim at the stairs as Tony sat in a puddle of Chad's blood while sobbing. Bill's surprised eyes stared up at them.

"Fuck this," Steve roared.

He ran to the bottom of the stairs and blind-fired three shots up the stairs. The only damage done was to the wall at the top and plaster dropped to the floor as Steve moved up. He had advanced halfway up the staircase when Tony got his attention.

"Don't go up there, man," he whined.

Steve shook his head; glad he was man enough to hold the gun at least. He returned to his ascent and realised an old man now stood on the top step. Steve's eyes stared down the barrels of the shotgun.

The boom made Tony flinch as Steve's body bounced off the bottom wall and landed near Bill's head. Tony began to weep sadly and looked down at his lap. Slow footsteps descended the stairs until they padded right beside him.

"Look at me," an elderly man's voice demanded.

Tony raised his head and stared in disbelief at the man who resembled a dusty cowboy. The man appeared relaxed as he replaced the empty cartridges in his double-barrel shotgun.

"This here was my daddy's," he told Tony. "He was a real mean son of a bitch, and he raised me to be the same."

Tony suppressed a whine which threatened to leap from his throat.

"You know who I am?"

Tony nodded as snot bubbled from his nose to mingle with his tears.

"Tell me," the man sneered.

"Erin's dad."

"That's right, I'm Erin's dad. She sent me a call via the satellite phone. Great investment those things, lemme tell you. So, as it goes, I raised my girl the same way I was raised."

Tony wiped his eyes and looked at the old man again.

"I raised my daughter to be a mean son of a bitch."

This amused the old man and he laughed until a chesty cough halted him.

"I can promise you that your boss, or best friend, whatever, is as dead as the rest of your sorry crew."

"Please don't kill me," Tony wept.

The old man looked around at the carnage of dead meat he'd left strewn across the floor, and then levelled the shotgun. Tony's face landed on the television screen like a pizza slice being thrown from a speeding car.

"We've been preparing for this my

whole life," he sighed.

NOTES

I refer to this as a reverse slasher. Which isn't as rude a concept as it sounds. I wanted to have a setup which paints our MC in a state of vulnerability, so we think she's going to be on the run from all the dangerous men who have been sent her way. Instead, we soon find they have picked on the wrong one. It's the hunter becoming the hunted horror edition. The concept was driven by my will to raise both my wonderful daughters to be strong and intelligent enough to cut through the increasing dangers of this crazy world. I'm no prepper or survivalist of course but it's a lot more fun to stretch the truth when writing fiction.

Opt-Out

The news had been a constant stream of paranoia which Joe and Kelly had been mainlining into their veins since the pandemic. Death, terrorism, and war sat in the forefront of their minds at all times. With no kids and no wish to travel a world which seemed poised to implode; the couple decided to invest their money elsewhere. They paid a specialist company to install an underground steel bunker in their back garden over a period of six months. The structure had air filtration, a separate water system, and the couple stocked it with tinned and dry food stuff. Joe worked for a large bank in the city; while Kelly was a graphic designer who was able to make a fortune from the comfort of their home. After one particularly stressful commute, Joe collapsed onto the sofa with his head in his hands. Kelly had been following the latest war in the east with morbid fascination while the cogs in her mind turned feverishly.

"We should use the bunker," she blurted

out to her husband.

Joe looked up wearily but couldn't help smirk at the suggestion.

"Like a sleep-over?"

Kelly walked over and sat down next to Joe. He saw the fatigue in his wife's eyes which resonated in his soul.

"You ok, baby?"

Kelly turned with a sudden spark of enthusiasm and launched into a speech she didn't even realise had been rehearsing itself in her mind.

"I'm tired, Joe."

"Let's have an early night then," her husband interrupted.

"That's not what I mean."

Joe looked perplexed but there was no stopping the flow of words which poured from Kelly's mouth. It felt like they were coming from her very core.

"Don't you just want a break from everything? Just opt out of the entire society shit show y'know? This world which just takes from us as it tries to destroy itself. There're millions of people out there but all I can feel is this hive mentality of loneliness. Like if we keep consuming and hating, then maybe we'll find happiness. All we do is work and then spend a few hours together."

Kelly grabbed Joe's hand and squeezed it sincerely.

"Those are the only parts of my life I still

love. I'm sick of feeling like we have to steal them from some unseen masters. The world has gone to shit and it's like nobody cares enough to mention it. I see you, Joe. I see how beaten-up work has got you and it breaks me."

Joe's eyes shimmered in response, so Kelly focused on his hand which she held tightly.

"We're literally watching the news for an excuse to escape to the bunker. I know you feel the same because when the installation was finished, it was the happiest I've seen you in years."

Joe wiped a stray tear away which surprised him with its rebellion.

"What about my job?" he sniffed.

Kelly knew her husband was already enjoying the thought of hiding from the world.

"We have enough saved to give ourselves a few months of breathing space afterwards. Plus, we'll barely be spending anything when we're down there. We have enough supplies to last us twelve months if we're careful."

"This is mad," Joe laughed with a snort.

Silence fell over the room and the pair looked at the candlelight which created ghostly shadows across the magnolia walls. Free spirits rebelling against bland conformity.

Maybe that could be us, Kelly thought.

Joe began nodding rapidly and gave Kelly's hand a squeeze in return.

"Yeah, let's do it."

The couple embraced and found themselves weeping openly as the floodgates of relief opened. Kelly had unlocked something hidden away in the back of Joe's mind. He'd been miserable for so long it had solidified as acceptance. Now they had a chance to turn their backs on the whole messed up system for an entire year.

"We're going to need a lot of books," Kelly laughed excitedly.

Six months later

The first three months had been everything they'd wished for. Their safe haven allowed them to leave their troubles outside while they reconnected to be the giggling teens who had fallen in love all those summers ago. Boredom was never going to be an issue as the pair played games, devoured books, and exercised together. Even the food was passable, and certainly a hardship of blandness the pair were willing to endure to stay hidden away. However, by the end of the fourth month, the cracks were beginning to show in the places the couple least expected. It had started with a conversation about what they thought was happening to the outside world and ended with Joe feeling a deep concern for the state of their finances once they left the bunker.

What if I can't find work?
What if we lose the house?
We'll lose the bunker too!

Kelly had hated herself for feeling the same shivers of dread about their future. A few weeks passed in the new subdued atmosphere before the couple sat and discussed the issue during supper time. They acknowledged the thought of staying in the bunker for the full twelve months was causing them the same amount of stress as what had put them in there in the first place.

So they decided six months was plenty and, if they were honest, had been a fantastic, shared experience which had helped strengthen their bond. It had been a relief to shed the guilt and know they were still on the same page.

Now though, as they stood in their house again, the euphoria drained from them like the steady drip of a neglected, leaking pipe.

"For fucks sake," Joe seethed.

Kelly scanned the ransacked lounge with tears in her eyes. The thought strangers had been going through their things disgusted and terrorised her in equal measure.

"I'll phone the police."

Kelly watched Joe pick up the phone and frown before checking the line.

"It's dead."

"Maybe we've been cut off?" Kelly tried.

Joe put the phone back in the cradle and scratched his beard.

"Na, there was more than enough in our account to cover any outgoing payments."

Kelly barely heard Joe's answer. She was too busy stepping through their discarded items and broken furniture. Whoever had been in their house had appeared to want to destroy everything rather than take it from them. Their television still sat on its stand, but its screen was badly cracked. Even the curtains had been ripped from their rails. Kelly held herself and worried that the scene seemed to acknowledge the wanton destruction had been personal.

"Absolute bastards," Joe groaned at his smashed record collection.

Kelly plugged their phones in to charge, and was relieved to see the battery icon appear.

"Well, we've not been cut off at least."

Joe gave his wife a rueful smile and put his arms around her protectively.

"You going to be ok if I nip to the store to get some supplies?"

Kelly looked out the front window at the sunny suburban day. Families went about their lives the same as they did before she had descended the steps to their bunker. It was all the reassurance she needed.

"Yeah, sure. I'll phone the police once my phone has enough charge."

Joe finally got their car started after

singing the praises of his automatic battery charger. Kelly sorted through the debris of their lives for a brief time until she was angry enough to make the phone call to the police. The fire in her belly fizzled out after five attempts resulted in a busy line. Kelly reluctantly opened the internet on her phone and checked the local news. No matter which site she tried, the latest news showed as being updated on February the fifth. Kelly frowned at the small device in her hand. Today was August the eighth. She restarted her phone and looked for any app update, but the same news showed on every available site. There was nothing out of the ordinary in the headlines for the fifth of February, and Kelly put her phone in her pocket feeling totally bemused.

A figure moved on her lawn which startled Kelly until she realised it was just Mike from next door. She went to the front door and opened it to the man who continued to look into their house via the big lounge window.

"It's a mess," Kelly called out to him.

For a moment it seemed like Mike wouldn't reply. It was as though he didn't want to acknowledge her presence. Finally, he turned and looked at her in a way which made Kelly feel defensive. His eyes betrayed contempt and his top lip curled in a display of anger.

"What do you expect?"

"Sorry?" Kelly was dumbfounded.

Mike took a few steps forwards and jabbed his finger in her direction.

"Leaving your house vacant like that. What do you expect, you idiot?"

"Excuse me? Don't call me an idiot!"

Mike bared his teeth like a rabid dog and tilted his head to one side as though he were about to play with his food.

"You're no better than me, bitch."

Kelly was so taken aback that she stumbled over her words. Her neighbour had always been pleasant and there had never been any disputes between them. Certainly, there was nothing she could think of which justified such vile comments.

"I'm glad they trashed your house," Mike muttered as he walked back across the lawn.

"Hey, wait a minute," Kelly called out. "What did you just say?"

Mike had already disappeared from view and Kelly heard a door slam shut.

She was beyond angry, but something about her neighbour's erratic behaviour forced her back inside.

Joe returned with no supplies and a badly damaged car. He was visibly shaken, and Kelly had to patiently withdraw the events from him like a troublesome splinter.

"I didn't get anywhere near the store," Joe confessed in a shrill voice.

Kelly wanted to talk about Mike but was

more concerned for her husband. She touched his face, and he flinched before continuing.

"A van ran into the back of me when I stopped at the lights on Laffak Street. I was going to get out, but they just kept accelerating. Thought it might be a road rage thing so I drove off as quickly as I could. Lost them after a bit and, and -"

Tears pooled in Joe's eyes, and he lifted a shaky hand to them.

"Joe? What happened, love?"

"A car rammed into the passenger side near the park."

"What?" Kelly gasped. "Another one?"

"Then another hit the rear again straight after," Joe said in a hollow voice. "I didn't think I'd get the car home."

Kelly threw her arms around her husband's neck and pulled him close. He wept into her chest, and she agonised over telling him about Mike's outburst.

As though sensing heightened tension in his wife's embrace, Joe pulled away and gave her a knowing look.

"Something happened here too," Kelly confessed.

She told him about the busy police line and the conversation with their neighbour.

"What's going on?" Joe had whispered like a child.

Presently, he was threatening to go and drag Mike from his home. Kelly recognised the posturing as her husband recovering from the fright of his aborted journey to the store and welcomed it. Joe marched across the lawn and banged on Mike's door with his clenched fist. He felt his breath leaving him in ragged adrenaline fuelled rasps. Nobody came to the door, so Joe banged on it again.

"Get out here, you fucking coward!"

Again, nobody came to answer but Joe could hear something from inside the house. He leaned towards the door and heard the sound of objects clattering to the floor as though being thrown. Joe put his ear against the door and scowled at a strange wailing sound from somewhere deeper in the house. Something scraped on the other side of the panel which forced him to stagger back in fright.

"Fuck this," he muttered and headed home.

*

They'd gone to bed in a state of confused frustration. The fact the news was stuck on the same date on Joe's phone as it was on her own filled Kelly with dread. Joe was too angry with Mike, as well as their inability to get through to the police, to discuss the issue, so Kelly dropped it. She knew her husband was scared too and so they both wriggled uncomfortably in the darkness of their bedroom. Both tried to ignore the nagging thought that they should have stayed in the bunker. Kelly had pulled the covers over her face to compensate for the proximity of the bunker which she craved. It was after midnight when Joe shook her awake. His face was eerily pale in the glow of the streetlight which leaked into their bedroom. Kelly sat up to try and fight against the disorientation.

"What's the matter?"

Joe looked over his shoulder. When he returned to Kelly, she was shocked by the screwed-up expression on her husband's face. It didn't belong to him because she'd never seen it there before. No, the terror which clung to him belonged in her nightmares.

Then Kelly heard it and realised the sound had been there from the moment she'd opened her eyes.

"What is that?" she muttered to the dull hum outside.

Joe escorted her to the window.

"Keep low, ok?" he said as he parted the curtains slightly.

Kelly looked at her man, reduced to a child, and then looked outside. Her stomach flipped in a rare way reserved for seeing a bad car accident or footage of a terrorist attack. The whole street was a moving river of people flooding past their home. They moved as one and in the same direction. Kelly saw people in their nightwear, some in a state of undress, and even a few naked bodies. She could see men, women, and children of all ages moving past. There were masses of staff from the nearby hospital as well as patients who stumbled by with bandages for clothes. Then there was the noise. Above the murmur from the crowds below there was a steady hum of something full of bass.

"What is that? Where are they going?" Kelly whispered.

Joe moved away from the window and put his hands to his face in despair.

"I don't know," he groaned. "I don't know what's going on."

Kelly let the curtain fall from her shaking hand and walked to Joe.

"Maybe we should see where they're going?"

Joe gave her a pained look of uncertainty.

"Things have been off since we came back out of the bunker, Joe. Don't you want to know what the hell is going on?"

Joe rubbed his face vigorously as though trying to wake himself from a bad dream.

"Yeah, you're right."

The pair dressed quickly and found themselves hesitating near the front door. It felt as though the mysterious noise was vibrating through the handle as Joe turned it. The waves of people meandered past, and the couple were relieved they were completely ignored by the masses. Kelly held Joe's hand and they fell in with the crowd. Nobody spoke and all had glazed eyes as though in a trance. The pair exchanged looks of fearful confusion, instinctively aware speaking wouldn't be a good idea. Joe occasionally stretched up so he could look over the heads of those nearest. Each time he was shocked with what appeared to be the entire community making their way towards the centre of town.

Kelly felt as though she were part of a strange, silent parade and the hum of noise was getting louder with every street they passed through. The crowd began to slow down as one just when the sound felt as though it were reverberating through the couple's bones. Joe grimaced and nodded to a space to the side of the crowd. Kelly followed until they were standing outside the shuttered front of a convenience store. Their eyes went from the masses gathering in the town square and wandered towards the town hall. Kelly gripped Joe's hand painfully at the sight waiting for them there. A black column had seemingly erupted through the concrete directly in front of the government building. Its surface looked like tinted glass, but it crackled with bright electricity which moved to the deep hum the crowds had been following. Joe followed its path to the night sky and looked away at the maddening way it stretched endlessly upwards blocking out the stars. The couple knew they were looking at something which was both ancient and not of their world.

The noise continued and Kelly wondered what had happened while they were in the bunker which had affected the community to render them in such a way. Where the Hell had the strange, endless tower come from. She looked at the faces of the crowd who were all mesmerised by the structure. The sound had seemingly created a hive-mind mentality which led them all towards it. Kelly thought about the change in her neighbour's behaviour and wondered if Mike was standing in the crowds with the same glazed expression.

"We need to get out of here," she whispered to Joe.

A nearby family of four turned in their direction before returning their stares to the tower. Joe gave Kelly a look of reproach about talking, so she tugged on his hand frantically and motioned with her head to indicate they needed to leave.

The dull noise from the strange tower suddenly cut out, leaving them both feeling as though their pulse was throbbing in their temples. A silence fell over them like a sheet of heavy fabric. Kelly began to back away from the crowds as quietly as possible which forced Joe to follow in fear of losing her. They were both stopped in their tracks by a heavy red glow engulfing the area. Joe turned and realised the strange structure had changed colour to a deep red. Once more, he was taken aback by the scale of the tower; which seemingly penetrated the night sky like a bloodstained sword. He felt the chill in his bowels as his primal subconscious warned him the threat level had increased.

"Kelly?"

His wife turned with a contorted face which showed she felt the same crushing weight of distress. A sound cut through the silence in the way a gale force wind moves inland from the seas. It was the aural equivalent of a rusty nail being scraped over endless sheets of glass. Both Joe and Kelly dropped to their knees as their nervous system scrambled for the control the sound had taken from them. Kelly clamped her eyes shut in agony and pressed against her ears until she felt as though the skull would give under the pressure. Joe slowly dropped face down on the ground until the concrete grazed skin from his forehead and chin. The pitch of the sound was so severe he felt as though it were compromising his eyesight as everything appeared to be reverberating around him. Even so, he squinted to the road at the crowds of legs of the masses who appeared to be completely unmoved by the sound. There was a moment when the noise escalated to the point the couple knew they couldn't take any more, and then it suddenly cut out.

Kelly moved to her husband and helped him up. The high-pitched sound was gone but it still haunted their eardrums which rang like alarm bells. They checked each over and Kelly stroked Joe's face affectionately. When they returned their gaze to the road, both flinched at the sight. Every single person in the crowd, man, woman, and child, had turned in their direction. Hateful sneers were their uniform. Kelly's eyes found a boy of around seven years old. He wore Spider-Man pyjamas and an expression of pure hatred towards her. Kelly shook her head to the hurt and confusion.

"Kill them!" a voice from the crowd exploded.

The couple took another step backwards before the initial cry became a chorus from every single person in the street.

"Kill them! Kill them! Kill them!" they all chanted.

Joe and Kelly ran for the nearest side-street without hesitation. Their flight response had overridden their bodies in the same manner the high-pitched sound had. Scrambled thoughts interrupted their burning lungs as they were chased across a huge shopping car park.

Where did the structure come from?
Why did we leave the bunker?
What's happened to everyone?

They had no time for answers as they ran for their lives. Mercifully, the dozens of discarded vehicles worked against the speed of the pursuing masses. Joe and Kelly weaved around them while the cars created bottlenecks for the crowds who had to negotiate them like turnstiles.

"Look!" Kelly shouted to Joe.

Joe saw the headlights beaming just up ahead which gave his aching legs one last shot of adrenaline.

A taxi had been abandoned by its owner, who was no doubt now part of the hordes chasing the couple. The driver door was open, and Kelly jumped behind the wheel. She accelerated before Joe had his legs safely inside, just as fists began pounding the car's bodywork. Joe braced so as not to fall out and managed to shut the passenger door. He shuddered at the sight in the wing mirror. The crowds were continuing their pursuit even as the taxi sped away.

"What the fuck is going on?"

Kelly didn't reply. She was too focused on swerving around the vehicles which the crowd had left behind. Metal skins shed for their strange pilgrimage. They made it a few hundred more metres before hitting a barrier of cars.

"Shit!" Kelly screamed as she beat her hands against the steering wheel.

"Come on," Joe huffed as he jumped out of the taxi.

They weren't far from home, and they

ran with all they had left. Distant cries of "kill them" followed them around every corner.

Joe ran around the side of the house and kicked the gate open. Kelly followed him to the hatch, and they hastily descended the ladders to their sanctuary. Both wept openly as they embraced and cast fearful glances at the locked hatch. The silence soothed them, and Joe walked to the food store to check on their supplies. He cursed himself for not doubling up and felt pangs of stupidity and guilt at having used six months of food already. Water wasn't going to be a problem, but they'd have to venture out for food sooner rather than later. He walked back to near the ladder where Kelly hugged herself nervously. Joe was about to mention the supplies when a sound came from the hatch. At first it sounded like the first splashes of rain on a caravan, but soon it developed into thunder. Kelly sobbed in anguish at the thought of the fists which beat against their only exit. Joe dropped to the floor, so he was sitting cross-legged with his hands clamped over his ears. They were trapped in the bunker, but this time the outside world was taking a keen interest in joining them.

NOTES

Have you ever wanted to just get away? Just remove yourself from society. Hard same, dear reader. Opt-Out wasn't written for anything particular. It was just a story that I had to commit to the page. I was frustrated about the world spinning straight from COVID into a lot of countries trying their best to start WWIII. Add into the mix, my frustration regarding the area I live in, and the money troubles which haunt so many of us and I had enough motivation for the story. I liked the idea of an event occurring while the couple were safe in their bunker, but that it doesn't reveal itself immediately. Things would seem just a little off at first before the real danger would reveal itself. I liked toying with the idea that their sanctuary would not satisfy their need to get away, and that ultimately it would become their tomb. In post-apocalyptic movies and games there are sometimes hidden areas where skeletons have been trapped and I often wonder what their story could have been. Well, Opt-Out is the story of the skeletons who thought they'd escaped.

A Child in the Shadow of God

With Sarah Jane Huntington

Every morning they caked her in the same mud they were forced to mine. From the moment Fajr was born, her parents knew she was special. Of course, to live in the depths of an Avaritian mine was to know that special things must be hidden. Years earlier, Fajr had exited the womb glowing like the moons. Her father, Lysander, had been terrified enough to throw mouldy blankets over the new-born to prevent the light alerting any nearby guards. Now though, the routine was always the same. Smother Fajr in dirt, wrap her in blankets, and put her in the carrying pouch her father wore on his back. As long as the parents were careful, the Avaritians gave the child nothing more than their usual look of disgust reserved for their slaves. As they left their ramshackle hut to three blasts on the worker's bugle; Glathkin thanked the stars for sending her a calm child who never cried or fussed.

Even so, she looked nervously from the

pouch on Lysander's sinewy back to the nearest Avaritian guard. Its reptilian eyes were busy watching the front of the work detail, otherwise Glathkin may have been beaten for such intrusion. Motherhood had galvanised Glathkin's spirit and brought a reckless streak to her usually fearful nature, so she openly looked the guard up and down. Strange muscles were poorly hidden under its military tunic, while long grey legs troubled its skirts. Avaritian skulls were rumoured to be small, yet layers and layers of mottled flesh made them appear bloated like corpses left too long in the seas of Jintau. Although Avaritian's came in all shapes and sizes, the smallest were always at least two feet taller than the largest Kintors.

Glathkin looked back at the bones which worked to the surface of her soul companion's starving body and closed her eyes to stall any escaping tears. After a time, she opened her puffy eyes and looked up at where the sky should have been visible. Instead, a network of Avaritian technology blacked out the view by creating an impenetrable cage which the invaders had trapped her tribe under many, many cycles ago. The enclosure ensured conditions remained forever dark like the environment on Avaritia, while the Kintor's were forced to mine the metals and minerals their slavers craved. Now, the only light was the haunting glow from the lanterns which marked the paths from the huts down the slopes into the mine. Glathkin allowed her mind to drift back to bright days on the farm where she'd been happy to work their fields and be amazed by the strength Lysander displayed. A painful shove rocked her head back and Glathkin released a cry of anguish.

"Move!"

Glathkin shuffled closer to Lysander before the guard felt it necessary to drag her away to the sheds.

"You must be careful, my love," Lysander whispered without taking his eyes from the cue ahead.

Glathkin nodded in agreement but then stole a glance at Fajr and felt the familiar surge of recklessness which her daughter emboldened in her.

Digging time moved quicker when Glathkin let her mind wander to whispered conversations she'd had with Lysander in their hut. Plans made and dismantled before the working day sneaked towards them once more. Glathkin was careful to keep an eye on Fajr in case her glow threatened to penetrate the mud and blankets; always on hand to apply more when the guards were busy beating a tiring slave. Lysander grunted as he worked with a tool he'd have to leave behind once finished. Sweat poured from him and his agony was accentuated by the weight of his firstborn. He clenched his jaw to the pain. Showing weakness meant death in this wretched, dark place and he wanted desperately to protect his family even if his body failed him each day.

"I had a dream, my love."

Lysander looked down at Glathkin as she scooped clay into a large bucket. She looked up suddenly to check if he'd heard her comment. His heart broke at her beauty and how it was wasted to the shadows of this hellscape. He responded by sinking the shovel further into the mud. A rock lay there, and his blistered hands ached from the shockwave which danced up the tool. Lysander dropped the shovel and fell to his knees to work out the stone with his hands.

"It was beautiful," Glathkin continued. "Our miracle child saved us from this place."

Lysander's head snapped around to her in response, but he yelped in pain before he could voice his shocked reply.

Both Glathkin and Lysander stared at the large wound as it wept blood into the mine. They both knew it meant death if any from Avaritia deemed him unfit to work. Glathkin tore from her shawl and wrapped Glathkin's hand as they exchanged looks of horror. There was no way they could hide the injury long enough for it to heal.

Back in the hut, Glathkin settled their daughter down onto the mound which resembled a nest more than a bed. As usual their angel did not so much as murmur. Lysander sat cross legged on the mud floor of their hut and stared morosely at his bandaged hand.

"Let me tell you of my dream," Glathkin tried.

"I know of your dream!" Lysander snapped a little too loudly.

Glathkin felt wounded but continued.

"I haven't told you all of it."

"You don't have to because I know how it ends."

"But how?"

Lysander looked up from his bloodied hand.

"Because I had the same dream last night."

Glathkin felt her knees buckle and suddenly she was huddled on the floor next to her man.

"Somehow I knew of it."

Lysander nodded sadly and appraised his wounded hand.

"It won't stop bleeding," he said almost to himself.

Glathkin stared at the father of her child in disbelief. Why was he fussing about his hand amidst a miracle?

"My love, we must make plans."

"What plans?" Lysander hissed.

Something heavy walking by their hut stunned them into silence. The dim glow from an energy lantern momentarily cast a bloated silhouette across one side of their hut. A paralysing sense of paranoia rooted the couple to the mud floor as they stared, eyes wide open, at the door flap. Glathkin envisioned a guard rushing through, impaling her and Lysander on the same lance. The figure stood outside for seconds, which masqueraded as minutes, before finally grunting and moving back into the darkness which swallowed it gleefully.

Glathkin was about to press home her point of making plans when Lysander dropped his head as though ashamed.

"I am scared," he whispered.

The tears came easily to Glathkin. Seeing her rock broken down in such a way was equally upsetting as it was terrifying. Lysander wiped his own tears away and looked across to where his daughter lay. Although the gloom within the hut was dense, he could have sworn Fajr was watching them.

"Whatever it takes, I will get you out of here."

Lysander turned to Glathkin and nodded to indicate he meant his words. He held his good hand out and Glathkin gave it a squeeze of sincerity.

"We must plan, my love."

Lysander nodded once more and looked over at Fajr to steel himself.

"We'll leave tomorrow night and follow the way of the dream."

***

They took only water with them. It sloshed chaotically in the wooden pail and the pair winced at the noise. Fajr sat alert in the pouch as though she knew the importance of their journey.

Did she dream of it too? Glathkin wondered.

They moved low and slow, using the network of huts as cover against the patrolling guards. If they were seen just once their whole family would be wiped out and Lysander felt a tension in his soul which threatened to crush him. His mouth was parched from it, so the sound of the water lapping at the pail was slow torture. Lysander gritted his teeth to the temptation. The water they carried was for a higher purpose than drinking. Glathkin pulled at his sleeve and the pair fell into a crouch beside one of the countless huts. Lysander cursed his concentration for not noticing the guard standing so close. The Avaritian stood between two huts with its back to them. Lysander wished for a weapon, but deep down knew the pits had taken too much of his strength for him to wield one effectively. The Avaritian began to turn and both Glathkin and Lysander closed their eyes as they awaited the roars which would precede their demise. A wretched bout of sobbing came from the nearest hut and the guard moved out of view to the front of it.

"Quiet, or I will drag you from there!"

Lysander scooted away as quickly as he dared with Glathkin close behind him. They zig-zagged around the workers quarter, using the deep shadows as cover against several patrols. Glathkin occasionally scouted ahead before appearing around a hut and motioning for Lysander to follow. All around them were the snores, whimpers, and sighs of their people, but the family pressed on with tunnel vision. Soon they reached the end of the camp where they could see the last of the threadbare woods. It was yet another sign the Avaritian's would use up all the area's resources until the lands were barren. The family understood that included their people too.

"We must move quicker now."

Glathkin nodded at Lysander as they looked at the open space between the huts and the woods. Without another word they broke for the trees. The air felt alive around them as though full of warnings, but somehow, they reached cover without being seen. Glathkin stole a look into the pail to see they'd lost half of the water. She prayed it would be enough.

They moved through the trees for what felt like hours. No light occupied the space so the pair had to grope past trunks and branches as best they could. Their faces were heavily slashed by the time they reached their destination. Lysander stopped and squinted into the murk. There lay only open ground before them, and he saw the ripple of something just ahead. Their people had a name for the cage which imprisoned them.

"It's the Shadow of God," Glathkin announced.

The hum of alien technology was audible at such proximity, and they knew touching the obstruction would reduce them to ashes. Lysander turned away from Glathkin to present Fajr to her mother. Glathkin dutifully extracted her daughter from the pouch and noticed the glow was beginning to penetrate the old dirt on Fajr's arms. She unwrapped the child like the gift she was, and Lysander joined her side to gently bathe Fajr in what was left of the water. The cloudier the water became, the stronger the glow came from the child's skin. Fajr's parents squinted at their task such was the brightness. Glathkin wept at her daughter's true beauty now she wasn't hidden under dirt and blankets. It was the first-time mother and father had seen Fajr as she was intended, and they sobbed and giggled in equal measure. They sat their daughter on a blanket when they had removed all the mud from her skin. Without hesitation, and just like in their dream, Fajr began to crawl towards the cage which had held their whole tribe captive for so long.

There was a crackle in the air and the wall of the cage appeared to ripple as though to the child's appearance. Glathkin took a step forward in nervous anticipation of Fajr getting dangerously close to the barrier. As if on cue, her daughter stopped crawling and rolled into a sitting position. For a moment Fajr closed her eyes as though about to sleep, but then the glow from her skin increased rapidly to an impossible brightness so that both parents were forced to turn from it.

"Fajr!" Glathkin screamed over the deafening noise the cage now made.

She turned to try and go to her daughter, but it was like looking into the sun of Drykos. The ground felt as though it were shaking from the vibrations the barrier was now producing. It was reacting more violently to the brilliant light Fajr was giving out. A huge crack ripped across the cage and Lysander gasped as he saw daylight on the other side. More cracks appeared as the vibrations in the earth became unbearable. Both Glathkin and Lysander dropped to their knees with their faces covered until a huge concussive blow knocked them both over. When they finally raised up, they turned to see Fajr was no longer glowing, and appeared to have the skin of a normal child. One which sat contently in the rays of the newly exposed sun.

"She did it," Lysander wept.

Glathkin felt cool, salty tears fall. Heavy with disbelief, she crawled towards her daughter, the new sunlight filled her sight and created a display of colourful prisms in her vision. The strangeness took her by surprise, she was used to the darkness and dread of the pits, bleak greys, and deep browns only.

"Fajr," she called, her voice quivering with emotion.

Dreams, visions, premonitions. Both she and Lysander witnessed a miracle, a path to find the way out, a guide placed inside their minds as they lay sleeping. Was it truly the end of suffering and enslavement? Could it really be? Was freedom their own once more? Fajr only sat and smiled, her pretty eyes wide with amusement and knowledge she should not possess.

The wind blew with calm grace, a sensation Glathkin had forgotten existed. With it came new sounds, cries, and screams. Noise travelling from the village and stolen by the breeze.

The workers? She guessed. Each one was seeing the glorious sun again for the first time in many years. The energy field, the wretched Shadow of God, was no more. Glathkin scrambled to her feet and reached for their saviour, their special daughter.

"My love!" Lysander cried.

The tones of his voice carried fear, thick desperation. A deep growl followed, loaded with threats and savage brutality. A guard, an Avaritian. There it stood, all strength and malignancy. Scaled, impenetrable skin and cold green eyes full of hate, a snarl on its twisted, grotesque features. A forked tongue whipped out and licked the air greedily. In one clawed hand, it held a weapon of energy, a baton graced with a pure beam of white fire used to murder or punish. Glathkin had seen the tool wielded many times and witnessed the agony it caused. Many Kintors carried deep scars because of it.

The guard walked forward on muscular legs and raised the vile weapon. She saw in its callous eyes the desire to hurt, the passion for violence. Their escape attempt would not be forgiven, Avaritians possessed neither compassion nor empathy.

"Lysander move!" Glathkin screamed.

Lysander did not. He only raised his arms in defence and braced for impact.

Fajr opened her mouth to scream but not a single sound sprang forth. No cry, no wailing, no terror. Her tiny fists balled up, her small toes curled, her face grew red, and her eyes showed sparks of wildfire. The guard stumbled, dropped its weapon, and held its ferocious hands over its pointed ears. The shouts of pain Glathkin expected from Lysander instead came from the Avaritian. It fell onto the hard ground with a thud and shook rapidly, blue coloured blood began to pour from its nose, mouth, and ears.

It's dying, Glathkin realised.

She felt no pity, no mercy, and no regret. Although she'd spent her life fuelled by kindness, she had none for the writhing creature, the invader before her. She only stared as its mottled skin began to smoke, hiss and crackle. Burning from a soundwave she failed to hear or from the harsh rays of the sun, it hardly mattered.

Let it burn, she thought. *Let it become ash.*

Glathkin turned her back and swept her daughter up into an embrace.

"Hush now, we're safe," she told her. She reached for her husband and pulled on his clothing sharply.

They needed to move, with quick stealth before other guards came.

"How did Fajr do that?" Lysander asked, both dazed and impressed.

"A sound, I think. A noise too high pitched for us to hear."

"It's not possible."

"And yet, it is."

On shaking legs, Glathkin stood. A short climb would hasten their escape. The valley around them dipped into a hollow with hills on all sides. The lands used to be rich green in colour and lush, full of life and vitality. She remembered the world as it was before *they* came, before the Shadow of God imprisoned them all, before they became slaves.

Together, an army of three, they climbed step by careful step, the ground rough and jagged beneath them.

"It's a miracle," Lysander muttered repeatedly. "It has to be."

"Yes, truly, but please, hurry."

Divine intervention, the universe, the old and most ancient one, fate, or maybe chance had arranged for a nemesis of the Avaritians in the form of Fajr. Balance had arrived, light to chase away the darkness. A positive force to combat the negative; love to defeat the hate. A cure for the poison of the slavers. Their daughter was hope, goodness, and purity. Evil dare not tarnish such beauty. Perhaps someday, after many generations had passed, the story of Fajr would exist as a bedtime tale. Children would hear all about her, offering thanks and gratitude. She would be an inspiration for all. If they could escape.

The top of the incline came into view, Glathkin longed to turn around but needed to focus on moving forward, craving only to see the glory of nature once more. She held her daughter close and pulled her husband, each step was becoming more painful but magnificent sights awaited. The reward would be worth the pain. She remembered running streams of cool water, wild forests of vivid colours. Life. Animals that scuttled around inside spitefully sharp bushes, pretty birds, and the lilac berries that once decorated thick purple trees. Sights Fajr would adore. They had to save her, above all else she must see glory, not the darkness and hate she was used to.

Yet glory is not what they saw.

The colours Glathkin yearned to see

were gone, missing entirely. The valley below, as far as the eye could track, was covered with Shadows of God, energy cubes, traps. Oppression ruled.

An ocean of prisons, a sea of endless misery.

"There must be a hundred!" Lysander gasped and gripped her hand tighter.

Glathkin could only sob. Shock turned her blood to the coldest ice. Their world, their beautiful home was destroyed. Cage after cage, village after village, encased and damned. The deep forest was burned and had long ago vanished. The fresh stream, cracked, dry and dead. Overhead, a slowly revolving ship of huge magnitude hung aimlessly in the sky and cast cruel shadows. All sharp spikes and metallic in appearance. It thrummed with power and malevolence. An Avaritian vessel, an invader.

"I did not dream this!" Lysander said as he fell to his knees, overwhelmed by sorrow.

"Nor I," Glathkin admitted, her heart broken and ripped to pieces.

Three souls against a legion of vileness. Impossible odds to beat. Cold realisation spread through Glathkin. The dream had been a warning. A curse, not a gift, a tease, and not a vision of hope. There was no way out and no chance. The world was not their own anymore.

"What can we do?" Lysander said. He

wrapped his arms around his wife and child and held them both tightly. "There has to be a way."

No way forward, no way back.

Glathkin gazed at their sweet child, an innocent, destined to live in a world of absolute damnation and worse. She would be viewed as an anomaly, a threat, a thing to fear. She would be snatched away and destroyed. All meaning would cease to be, existence would be pointless.

Standing on the high hill, with nothing but sharp rocks below, Glathkin wondered if she should jump. Death might be the only true escape for them all. A plummet down into oblivion. Rather sharp rocks greet them than the claws of the Avaritians.

"Lysander," she whispered. "There is nothing but hopelessness ahead."

"We mustn't give in, stay strong my love. Look how far we've come and…"

Glathkin turned instinctively and gasped. Below was a landscape of dirt and tiny wooden huts. Hollowed out pits and a labyrinth of mines. A hole in the ground filled with the murdered or fallen; the frail or unable was stark and visible. But there were frantic movements, and furious battles taking place. Sounds of triumph. The villagers, the people they'd worked and toiled alongside for years, were fighting for their lives, and winning.

Several Avaritian guards lay dead,

stabbed, or beaten. Many workers in fierce groups carried the energy weapons that meant dread and pain. Roles had been reversed.

"The Shadow of God fell. The villagers are rebelling!" Lysander cried in amazement. Now tears began to fall again, happy tears.

People, in the face of evil, always found a way to defeat such savagery. A view of the sunlight above became the force needed and provided the distraction to act.

"No more, no more," was the chant they could hear. An uprising, slaves were becoming masters. Misery and fear had switched for intolerance and bravery. Many people were sprinting towards them, racing to join them, running to make a stand. Quickly, they were circled and protected, shielded. No, of course it wasn't over. It was only just beginning. The one they sought to protect and save, their daughter, was the one who would break the chains of them all.

Glathkin held the hand of Lysander, her love, and smiled.

"Ready?" he asked.

"Yes," Glathkin answered. "Yes, I am."

One by one they would cause the Shadows of God to fall. Freedom for those inside was inevitable. The world really would become their own once more. Hope must never be lost. Salvation had arrived.

"Ready little love?" Glathkin asked their daughter.

Wrapped in her dirty rags, Fajr began to giggle. Fajr began to glow.

NOTES

Are you a fan of Sarah Jane Huntington? Me too! So, you can imagine my excitement when Sarah agreed to write a story with me. Sarah was actually the first writer who read and reviewed my debut (The Cursed Caves). It was a real shot in the arm for me and I can't underestimate how much of a boost it gave me. I hope she knows that. We've gone on to read all of each other's books and I can't recommend them enough to lovers of horror and sci-fi. Working with someone of Sarah's talent and attitude made the whole experience effortless. We quickly found our styles were compatible and there were no disagreements whatsoever.

Anyway, onto the story. We didn't end up submitting it to the call which had actually prompted me to ask Sarah in the first place! Basically, what happened is we had so much fun writing the story, I asked Sarah if she would consider doing a collaborative collection with me. Five of her stories and five of mine, with A Child in the Shadow of God in the middle. Alas, it wasn't meant to be. There just didn't seem to be the time and Sarah withdrew from writing and social media for totally understandable reasons. So, this collection with its two collaborative stories is as close as I could possibly get to the original project. I exchanged emails with Sarah to seek her permission and of course she was her usual supportive self and told me to go for it.

The concept for the story was of my making, but nobody could have finished it like Sarah did. As usual we're taken from despair to hope a number of times before the end, and Sarah's style is unmistakable for any fans. It was my first attempt at writing dark fantasy, and although it probably shifted more towards sci-fi, I'm happy with how it turned out. I know Sarah is supportive enough to be reading this right now, so I just want to say thank you. From the support to the experience of sharing a story with you, many thanks.

Even Gatekeepers Die
With Sarah Jane Huntington

Abigail was one of the few town elders, an
important role she adored. There were
three in total, a trio, a trinity that acted with
fairness for the good, and the well-being
of a community of fifty souls.
It wasn't always plain sailing; some decisions
were beyond tough to make. She often
found she had to be cold and ruthless. A trait
that surprised others.
On the outside, she appeared happy, friendly,
and full of laughter. Her curvy body
and pretty black skin made her seem
appealing to every eye and gender. Yet
underneath, she could be cold and calculated.
Two sides, one coin.
Customers flocked to her bookstore during
the tourist season. Her shelves were
filled with antique, collectible books, most of
which she'd read several times and
hated to part with. Knowledge of all manner
of subjects was her passion; particularly
global myths and legends.
Still, she made a killing in sales every summer,

the whole town did.
Mostly, people visited for the organic foods
the town of Serpent's Lair grew so well.
Lush, exotic fruits, and huge prize-winning
vegetables, the very best around.
Although, some people came to see the
winding remains of the Serpent's mound
itself, a site of wonder and historical
significance.
She couldn't blame them; it truly was a
beautiful view to behold. Once, it lured her
into the town too.
She placed the last book back on the dusted
shelf and assessed her surroundings. It
was almost sunset and almost time.
She briefly closed her eyes and hoped the
night would run smoothly and without
chaos. Success never occurred by accident,
only by design.
Around her, the atmosphere was humming.
Static electricity or unknown energy was
present, ripe with anticipation.
Yes, the time was very close indeed. Here the
townspeople came with their long
lilac gowns and hoods. She moved quickly
and pulled her own gown off a rack. The
old traditions were important.
The first stirrings of excitement began.
Abigail was part of something magical,
wonderful in fact. A hive mind with the gift of
independent thought, a contradiction, a
collective, a mystery without end.

She lit a single white pillar candle in the window of the bookstore and held up a single hand to signal those standing outside. Wait.

As an elder, it was her privilege to make sure everything was in place before the inner sanctum was filled, and worship started.

She pulled back a thick Persian rug and unlocked the trapdoor, long ago built into the wooden floor.

Abigail smiled. What an honour and it was hers this year.

She carefully descended down.

The walls were rock, damp and cold. Her breath turned to steam and her teeth chattered rapidly.

"It's me, Abigail," she called out. "It's only Abigail."

Thirteen steps down, unlucky for some, that's all it took to enter a completely different world that no one but the townsfolk knew existed. An underworld without Hades or a ferryman to guide the way. An alien netherworld beneath their feet.

The thin door at the bottom of the steps creaked open at the first push and revealed a large, cavernous chamber. Stalagmites grew from the rocky ground like obscene growths or wild infections without a cure.

To a stranger, the path would appear hazardous and quite impossible. To her, she walked with ease, she knew the way and she

could feel the direction too. A lure, a
pull too compelling to ignore.
Across jagged rocks and dangers, she passed
easily until the stone-lined, deep well
came into view.
Its home.
Some called it the well of immortality, which
it was, in an odd way, and yet it
contained no magical spring water, no
ambrosia or nectar of the gods. Far from it.
Others who had walked the path called it a
hole to the centre of Earth. Old Nancy,
another elder, called it the birthplace of
monsters, the entrance to Hell itself.
Abigail arrived at the formation, the deep dark
hole, and waited. She need not be on
her knees, yet.
She knew it was there, watching and waiting
in that ruthless way it was prone to,
thinking, absorbing, deciding.
She closed her eyes. It was important not to
show fear. Being afraid seemed to
make It excited.
"I'm here," she whispered and listened to her
own voice echo.
She heard the sound of hissing first. A
powerful tone of hunger and menace. Next
came the smell, all sulphur, and rancid decay.
She braced for impact. No matter how many
times she witnessed the impossible
being, parts of her mind refused to accept
what it was she was seeing and

threatened to unravel.
Through her careful learning, and studies, she
knew the creature was more than
ancient. Superior in ways no mortal could
comprehend.
The Hindus called such creatures Naga.
Echidna in ancient Greece. Basilisk in
Europe. Mehen in Egyptian. Ningishzida in
Sumerian culture. Silurian. The Horned
Serpents, Reptilians, Dragon beings, snake
gods, and goddesses. A remnant of a
race long ago forgotten, a survivor of a world
from before, or something else entirely.
A being with a thousand or more names and
identities.
Every culture, every nation on earth possessed
some version of it, stories of their
own and forbidden knowledge handed down
by word of mouth and shared secrets.
Modern-day people discarded such myths as
frightening tales told in the dark and
nothing more.
Abigail once believed the same. Until she
discovered the town of Serpent's Lair and
found the truth almost one hundred and
eleven years ago to the day.
No outsider would guess her true age, no one
would believe she had been chosen
and blessed by divinity.
She heard movement, dry scaly flesh rubbing
against rock and stone. She opened
her eyes and as always, staggered back with

shock.

It, she, he, not one soul in town knew. They only knew It needed to be fed in order to spread its influence and bless them all with the gift of prolonged life and perfect harvests.

A lost culture built a serpent design over its home, as a sign, marker, or warning not to trespass. But people had, of course, people always do. Curiosity can kill or bless.

The mass of its body filled the hole it slowly emerged from. Its skin appeared dull and would remain so until it fed and became shiny like glitter. Each scale that graced its flesh was the size of her hand, brown and dark green in colour and shimmering slightly, pulsing. It reared back like a cobra about to strike and assessed her. Abigail gazed straight back.

She was an ally, a friend, and part of the congregation meant to serve.

Its large face resembled a human, in part. Two narrow yellow eyes with slits for pupils, one stub-like nose, and a wide mouth filled with prominent fangs and sharp teeth. The way it moved, and swayed, felt magical and elegant. Hypnotic. Otherworldly. Beautiful.

Even if Abigail were blinded, and unable to see, she would still understand Its glory, Its unlimited energy.

Its presence filled the chamber with magnetic

power. It knew her, and she knew It. To both her shame and pride, she was loyal and devoted. A servant to the serpent.

"It's almost time," she managed to say. Like many before her, It had become her needy god, spreading its influence into her dreams and waking moments, giving her gifts, and accepting her admiration.

A thick forked tongue shot out and licked her cheek.

Yes, even through her fear, they were bonded tightly. The town and its inhabitants gave her shelter during hard times many decades ago. When people with black skin like her own were viewed as the enemy, they took her in because It called to her, It wanted her.

Abigail understood what it was to feel rejected, misunderstood, feared, and treated with scorn, and violence. To be different.

"We have two for you tonight," she said and raised her hand to touch the creature.

The hissing stopped and swapped for a soft crooning sound that felt like warm music on a soft wind.

"It won't be long," she continued. "And we'll be back with your meal. I came to check you were awake."

Down in the strange hidden chamber, the two entwined and embraced, a twisted kind of worship.

"Everything will be fine and then you can

sleep once more."
Abigail wondered if it dreamed. She believed
it absorbed people, swallowed them
whole yes, but stole their memories and
knowledge too. A study.
For what end, she did not dare to guess.
From above, a siren began to sound. The one
the town reserved for an incoming
tornado.
"It's time," she said very softly and stepped
away. "I won't be long."
An unpleasant job faced her, but in the death
of only two others, fifty-two and It
found new life and meaning.
Some sacrifices were worth making but every
year it became more difficult to kidnap,
lure or promise outsiders, and suspicions were
growing fast.
People went missing every year without fail in
the town, around the same date.
Spiteful rumours were changing into
investigations and facts. The worry gnawed at
her bones.
Last year, two lingering tourists had been
drugged and sacrificed. Outsiders,
authorities, came to ask tough questions that
were answered with smooth lies.
There were no bodies, no clues, and no hope
of finding any.
This year, two more had been snatched. A
fool's errand but an essential one.
What would happen if It wasn't fed? No one

with a working mind wished to find out. Abigail retraced her steps with haste and walked steadily up the stone steps, trying to fill her mind with the clarity she needed. The door flew open before she arranged her thoughts. Williams, the third elder. His expression was sheer terror. Immediately, her stomach plummeted.

"We've got a problem," he said. "A big fucking problem."

Williams and Abigail burst into the storeroom where a couple were bound, gagged, and flanked by hooded locals.

"Show me."

Bob, who owned the hardware store they stood in, came forward. He held out a police badge and Abigail's eyes glanced at the letters.

"Detective Jacob Murray. Monroe Police Department."

She glanced over Bob's shoulder and Jacob began to shout muffled obscenities through the duct tape. Blood trickled from a gash on his eyebrow. Things were going south, but Abigail knew her duty as an elder was to stay composed for the sake of the other townsfolk.

"The girl?"

"Wife."

"This doesn't change anything," Abigail announced to the room.

Williams arrived at her side and leaned in close and whispered.

"There's more."

"Go on."

Williams produced a mobile phone from beneath his gown.

"He managed to send off a message before we could drag him out of the motel bathroom."

"Jesus Christ. Any idea who?"

Williams nodded gravely.

"Reading their earlier messages, it looks like it's his work partner."

Abigail felt suddenly clammy and wanted to scream until her lungs grew raw. Yet, the room watched her and waited for her to lead. She put her hands on the curves of her hips and smiled warmly at those dressed in lilac.

"We have to assume the cops are on their way."

The room began to murmur, and the bound couple's eyes blazed at her in fury. Abigail continued before panic set in.

"Monroe is an hour away, so the only thing that changes is we must hurry. It is awake and it must feed."

"What of the police?" Bob groaned.

"Nothing can get in the way of the feeding. Nothing."

Hooded figures began to nod in agreement.

"Ben, I want you to get rid of their car. It might just buy us some time. "

Ben rushed out of the door with a swish of his gown.

"The rest of you prepare the feast and meet

me at the bookstore as quickly as you can."

***

Detective Keyshia Gibson sped her Dodge Charger down the rural roads towards Oak Springs. The car was squealing around the bends because of the message she had received an hour earlier from Detective Jacob Murray.

Hooded group attacking our room kidnap? help

She'd taken her leave at the same time as her honeymooning partner because he was her best friend and work sucked without him. Their colleagues made a whole host of inappropriate comments which the pair agreed was not only based on their opposing genders but also because people were still weird about friendships crossing invisible race boundaries. After receiving Murray's message, Gibson had sent an immediate alert. The operator had relayed an issue with contacting local law enforcement in Oak Springs but assured Keyshia that units from neighbouring Westcreek were on their way.

Now, she clinged to the hope she could save Jacob and Stacey from whoever the Hell had arrived in their room in the middle of the night. Keyshia was so in her own head, she almost collided with a white SUV which tore across the intersection. The brakes squealed like horses, and she snapped her head to the side to follow the SUV's trajectory. Keyshia's heart almost leapt from her chest. Not because of the close call but because the licence plate confirmed the car belonged to her partner.

"Motherfucker," Keyshia muttered as she threw her car into drive.

Her police training soon had Keyshia's Dodge catch the SUV up as it barrelled down a narrow road. The suspension was blasted by the bumps in the surface and it was difficult to see who was driving Jacob's car. Keyshia squinted and just about made out the driver who was wearing a large hood. Although the Dodge was unmarked, it was obvious she was pursuing the SUV, and the driver reacted by manoeuvring more erratically. Detective Gibson thought about backing off in case Jacob and Stacey were being forced to lie down in the back of the SUV or stowed in the trunk. The thought was erased by the screech of tires which signalled the hooded driver had lost control. Keyshia slowed slightly and watched in horror as the SUV fishtailed before leaving the road. She slammed the brakes on just as Jacobs' vehicle collided with a large tree.

White smoke hissed from broken pipes as Keyshia stalked down the embankment. She clutched her Glock 19 in both hands and let it lead her to the driver's side of the SUV. The door flung open, and Keyshia braced. After a short delay, a man in his early thirties half fell out of the car and leaned his back against the open door. Keyshia saw the blood dripping from the man's badly broken nose and watched in what felt like slow-motion as he reached behind him.

"Put your fucking hands where I can see them!"

The man pulled at something in his waistband and Detective Gibson fired off two quick shots from her service pistol. One bullet hit the man in the hip and ricocheted into the interior of the car, while the other went straight through his stomach and into the door behind him. He immediately sagged to his knees with a wide-eyed look of shock.

"Why'd you do that?" Keyshia yelled at him as he keeled over.

She rushed to him and quickly glanced into the empty SUV. A small knife lay in the grass next to the man.

"Where are they?" Keyshia asked as she patted the man down.

The man groaned as though he'd been hit in the stomach by a heavyweight boxer. Keyshia grabbed his jaw with one hand and pressed the Glock to the man's temple with the other.

"Detective Murray and his wife. Where are they?"

The man relaxed in her arms.

"No, no! Why'd you take them? Where you got them?"

The man began to talk in a whisper, so Keyshia leaned in.

"Feeding time. Under Oak Springs - must

feed."

The man convulsed once and died. Keyshia jumped and ran to her car. She'd call in the incident once she had her partner and his wife safe.

The Dodge idled as Detective Keyshia Gibson scanned the main centre of Oak Springs. It appeared to be a ghost town with drawn curtains and bolted doors. Hers was the only car on the road. The motel had been empty with a handwritten closed sign being the only trace of life. Keyshia removed the keys from her car and shoved a spare ammunition clip into her trouser pocket. It hung too heavy in a stark warning of its abilities. She moved quickly to a hardware store which was the nearest building. A pull on the door handles confirmed it too was locked. Keyshia pressed her face to the glass but couldn't see anyone inside. There was a sudden rumbling sensation below her feet as though the whole world was vibrating. Keyshia gasped and staggered from the doors. The ground suddenly stilled.

Earthquake?

Then the words of the hooded man came back to her.

"Under Oak Springs - must feed."

Sirens approached and Keyshia eyed the Westcreek patrol car speeding towards her. She sighed as any element of surprising Jacob and Stacey's attackers ebbed away. A man with an ill-fitting uniform and a crooked moustache

174

jumped out of the passenger side of the squad car.

"Drop the weapon!"

"Are you fucking kidding me? Turn the siren off you idiot!"

"Ma'am I will not ask again."

"I called this in! I'm Monroe P.D!"

The driver mercifully switched the siren off and Keyshia took a breath. She gestured at the badge which hung from a chain around her neck. The deputy squinted, but kept his gun trained on her. The driver door opened, and an older man stepped out.

"Lower your weapon, Dixon."

"But-"

"Now!"

Dixon flushed red and lowered his weapon. The older man nodded at Keyshia.

"Detective Gibson, I assume? I'm Sheriff McKenzie."

Keyshia's blood was up, and she had no time for pleasantries.

"Is anyone else coming?"

The Sheriff and his deputy looked at each other, wounded.

"There's been a bad collision up on Thorpe point," the Sheriff jerked his thumb over his shoulder. "All the patrolmen are up there dealing with absolute carnage from what I hear."

Keyshia rubbed her brow with her free hand.

"A detective and his wife are missing!"

Sheriff McKenzie rubbed the greying stubble on his square jaw as he pulled a face somewhere between hurt and angry.

"Then I guess we'd better start knocking on some doors."

No sooner than the words were out of his mouth, than a hail of bullets began to rain down from across the street. Buckshot and small rounds pinged off the patrol car like deadly hail. Keyshia saw deputy Dixon's throat split open as she dived for cover behind bags of topsoil. She heard him gurgling as she and the Sheriff returned fire. Across the street was the first open door Keyshia had seen since arriving in town. Three figures cloaked in lilac robes crouched there and shot in her direction. *What the Hell is going on in this town?* She thought as she crawled around to the deputy.

Dixon was completely still and the colour of his hands indicated he was past saving. Sheriff McKenzie had managed to get into cover behind his car and a salvo from his pistol dropped one of the men in the doorway. He fell face down as though a switch had been released. Keyshia stayed in a crouch and moved to the Sheriff's side. Glass erupted all over them, forcing them behind the car's bodywork. "Jesus fucking Christ. Jesus fucking Christ," the Sheriff said again and again.

Keyshia heard rushing feet and reacted quickly by swinging around and putting two bullets into the chest of the man who'd tried to flank them. Sheriff McKenzie raised up but jerked back as though he'd been tased. Keyshia looked down to see his right hand had been split almost in two by a bullet. The Sheriff put it under his left armpit as though trying to keep it warm and looked over sadly at his deputy lying dead in the road. He retrieved his gun from the concrete with his left hand and fixed Keyshia with eyes which watered with the agony of remaining conscious.

"They're holed up in the bookshop," he winced. "I can cover you so you can get to the side of it."

Keyshia nodded in agreement just as bullets thudded into the hood of the car. She was about to move off when the Sheriff called her back.

"There's a twelve gauge in the car. Fully loaded."

Keyshia pocketed her Glock and retrieved the shotgun. The shooting from the bookshop intensified as though they thought she were trying to escape.

"Now!" Sheriff McKenzie screamed and began firing into the doorway.

Keyshia held her breath as she sprinted across the road. A bullet zipped inches from her shoulder, but she made it across. She edged along with her back against the wall to get closer to the bookshop. Sheriff McKenzie was still firing and she heard splintering wood and a groan from the doorway. The shooting from the car stopped suddenly and when Keyshia looked back, all she could see of the Sheriff was his legs sticking out from behind cover. She scrunched her eyes closed and gritted her teeth. "Fuck these guys."

Keyshia moved to the doorway from the side. The moment one of the gunmen leaned out, she pulled the trigger. A shredded lilac gown flew through the air with the dead man as Keyshia pumped the shotgun. She heard scurrying feet from inside the store; she hurried into the doorway and pulled the trigger. The round caught the man square in the back which sprayed clots across the nearest shelves. Keyshia pumped a round and stepped inside but was immediately hit from behind which sent her reeling into the counter. The shotgun came loose from her grip, so she pulled the Glock from her waistband as she rolled to meet her attacker. Three bullets hit the woman who fell dead into her lap. Keyshia rolled onto her side at the sound of wood creaking. She watched in amazement as a trapdoor slowly opened to reveal the head and shoulders of another hooded man. Without hesitation, she squeezed the trigger of her pistol and watched brain and skull fragments wash up the inside of the trapdoor. The man's body disappeared with a slam of wood. Keyshia rushed over and hefted the trapdoor open and aimed the Glock. All she could see were stone steps and splashes of the man's blood. A bullet tore into the trapdoor near her hand, so she unloaded her clip into the darkness. After the echoes died away, she heard the thud of someone falling to the ground.

After waiting in silence for a few minutes, Keyshia slowly made her way down the steps. There was an unnatural coldness in the passageway which she could feel in her toes. A faint flicker of candle-light danced on the stone walls in the distance and Keyshia held out the shotgun and moved towards it. She could hear whispers in a foreign tongue and the passageway seemed to throb with every word. By the time Keyshia got to the entrance where the light came from, the passageway was practically humming. The route across was dangerous and twice Keyshia nearly fell onto sharp rocks below, but finally entered a chamber filled with a terror which immediately pulled at the edges of her sanity. At the rear of the large space lay a huge well and from it spilled something resembling a mix between a dragon and an anaconda. It was five times bigger than any similar creature she'd ever seen in pictures. To Keyshia's bulging eyes the thing was a demon rising up from her nightmares. She took in its yellow eyes, enormous scales, and giant fangs which dripped with a creamy looking fluid. Keyshia raised the shotgun before she lost her nerve.

"No!" Abigail screamed. "You can't, you can't!"

Keyshia watched the hysterical woman run between her and the beast. Then her eyes took in the lilac gown and she cuffed Abigail to the floor. Hissing erupted from the serpent and it began to sway erratically in its agitation. Abigail wiped blood from her lip and looked up imploringly.

"Please, you must leave here now."

"Fuck you, where are my friends?"

Abigail shot a quick nervous glance towards the creature.

"Please don't..."

Keyshia followed the glance and noticed the bulge in the serpent's body. It was swollen and human shaped. A flash of Jacob and Stacey's faces flashed to her mind and Keyshia screamed in fury and began firing the shotgun again and again as the echoes of her twisted bellow returned to her as something ungodly.

Abigail screamed too, but hers was a sound of grief and sorrow. The serpent swayed hopelessly as the shotgun tore lumps from its brown and green body. It reeled until it became limp and slowly slipped down the well until it was completely out of sight. Keyshia dropped the shotgun which clattered among the stalagmites.

"What have you done? What have you done?" Abigail wept below her.

Keyshia fixed the older woman with a look of murderous intent. However, before she could act on it, a chaotic bedlam erupted from the giant well. It was screams and howls mixed with the brass and drums of the dead. The whole chamber shook so that debris began to fall all around.

"You've doomed us all!" Abigail roared. "It was the only thing capable of guarding the gateway."

As if on cue, an impossibly long hand gripped the top of the well. It was clear and Keyshia could see black blood pumping through it. She didn't want to see what manner of demon was pulling itself to the surface, so turned and ran.

"You've killed us all!" Abigail wailed behind her.

Keyshia was near the trapdoor when she heard the woman let out an ear-piercing shriek of agony.

The detective didn't stop running until she was back at her car. As she lowered herself into the driver's seat, she saw strange lights blasting through the bookshop. The ground rumbled and the building fell in on itself so that the odd colours were thrown skywards. Keyshia gunned the Dodge so it screeched away and past the bodies of the Sheriff and his deputy. In the rear-view mirror she saw winged beasts moving out in all directions as giant insectoids scurry across the roads. Flames erupted in all directions and rained down with blood from the ashen sky. She blinked the terror away until she saw the older woman in the reflection.

"What have you done? What have you done?"

THE END (OF EVERYTHING)

<u>NOTES</u>

Due to the positive experience of our first collaboration, Sarah and I jumped at the chance to work together again. The call was for two writers to work together to create a horror story with particular characters. Sadly, the publishers called it a day due to reasons out of their control. This time Sarah started the story, and I wrote the second half. Our sides were written completely before we meshed them together and it was surprising to see how little we had to change for continuity etc. It was just another example of how similar our styles could be at times. Sarah created some wonderful characters, and I enjoyed throwing them into action with my usual carelessness. I wanted the end to be exactly that. An end to all things. Maybe Sarah should have written the second part and then at least there would be hope. Is the title a stab at various members of the writing community? Yes, of course it is. We're all equal here. It's just that some people never read the memo.

EDITORS NOTE: READ SARAH JANE HUNTINGTON

Not a Good Fit at This Time

Acknowledgements

I am nothing without the love and support of my family. Laura, you are my favourite beta reader/listener thank you for your belief, enthusiasm, and patience. To my warrior daughters Ava and Riley, I hope I'm making you half as proud as you make me every single day.

Special thanks to Damien Casey. A talented writer who has become a good friend. I won't forget all your help to make Below Economic Thresholds and this collection become a reality.

Here's a list of friends, writers, and content creators who have consistently supported my endeavours while remaining charitable towards my dry and sarcastic personality. You've all lifted me when I needed it and I hope I have done the same for you at some point.

Sarah Jane Huntington (obviously), Coy Hall, Mark Robinson, Austrian Spencer, Wayne Fenlon, Elford Alley, Kev Harrison, Dan Howarth, BP Gregory, Angel &Tasha, Wendy Dalrymple, S.J.Krandall, Jennifer Bernardini, Every single Pen on Twitter especially Pen of

Horror, Yolanda Sfetsos, Catherine McCarthy, Sarah Budd, Ronald McGillvray, Daniel Lorn, Joe Ortlieb, Brian G. Berry, Julie Crook , Linda Bromilow, Tony Jackson (who has died in at least two of my books).
To the readers and reviewers, thank you for your invaluable support. You keep me going back to the keyboard on a mission to improve with every release.

Printed in Great Britain
by Amazon

43336358R00106